CRASH INTO YOU

A Dare With Me Novel

J.H. CROIX

This is a work of fiction. Names, characters, businesses, places, events and incidents are either the products of the author's imagination or used in a fictitious manner. Any resemblance to actual persons, living or dead, or actual events is purely coincidental.

Cover design by Najla Qamber Designs

Cover photography: Sara Eirew

Reader's note: The early chapters of Daphne & Flynn's story were previously available for free in A Little Bit Cupid - an anthology of romance shorts published and available for a limited time through Lady Boss Press in February 2019. This is the full novel and complete story.

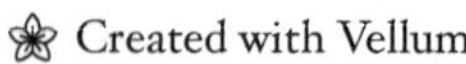 Created with Vellum

CRASH INTO YOU

A hotshot pilot and a Southern princess looking for a fresh start collide in the wilds of Alaska.

The first time I met Daphne involved three things: a cute skirt, a bear, and mud. Lots of mud.

Daphne is everything I don't need, and she makes me crazy in *all* the wrong ways. This princess does not belong in the wilderness. Or, so I think. But then, thought is hard to come by around Daphne.

Between flying tourists all over Alaska's skies, hotshot firefighting on the side, raising my sixteen year old sister who has enough attitude to run the world, and fending off demons from my days in the military, I don't have time for women.

But time's been laughing at me ever since Daphne showed up. I can't get her out of my mind, and my control has fled the building. Oh, and I'm her boss.

One night, just one night, I let things go too far. Now, all bets are off.

"Some people care too much. I think it's called love." -A.A. Milne

Sign up for my newsletter for information on new releases & get a FREE copy of one of my books!

http://jhcroixauthor.com/subscribe/

Follow me!
jhcroix@jhcroix.com
https://www.bookbub.com/authors/j-h-croix
https://www.facebook.com/jhcroix
https://www.instagram.com/jhcroix/

Chapter One

DAPHNE

A moose lumbered across the road in front of me, and I came to an abrupt stop, the SUV jerking when I slammed my foot on the brakes. "Holy shit!"

No one was in the SUV with me to hear my irreverent reaction. Although I'd done some research and knew wildlife was abundant in Alaska, it was still rather startling.

While the moose appeared to be moving slowly, its long stride covered the ground at a deceptively quick pace. Inside of a few seconds, the animal had crossed the road into a field abloom in fuchsia flowers. Its rump disappeared into a cluster of evergreen trees. I gave my head a small shake and realized I was stopped in the middle of a highway. It wasn't exactly busy, but nonetheless, it *was* a highway.

Laughing to myself, I eased off the brake and put my foot on the gas pedal again. Alaska's roads weren't crowded. As I glanced to the side while picking up speed, my breath caught at the ocean glinting under the sunshine splashing across its surface.

To one side of this highway was mountains and

trees, and to the other was Cook Inlet, stretching inland from the Pacific Ocean into Alaska. I'd already counted two glaciers and marveled at the way the ocean lapped at the base of the mountains on the other side as I drove along.

My GPS wasn't being too helpful. And I'd quickly discovered that the cell reception wasn't great here either. It was spotty at best and seemed only decent when I passed through the small towns scattered along this highway, which could take me to the farthest western point in the United States if I followed it that far.

"Dammit," I said as I glanced at the GPS on my dashboard screen.

The marker on the map still showed me sitting in a parking lot in Anchorage. "Please don't tell me you're broken."

I wished the friendly computerized voice would assure me she was not, in fact, broken. But she—the GPS voice in this SUV I'd rented, that is—remained stubbornly silent at my plea.

"Thanks for nothing," I muttered.

Anxiety, the worst kind of close friend, tightened in my chest. For the past year and a half of my life, I felt as if I'd been flung off a cliff with nothing in sight. I still felt as if I was spinning helplessly, trying to find a sense of equilibrium and somewhere to land. The last thing I needed was to get geographically lost rather than being metaphorically lost in my mind and heart.

"It's okay," I assured myself. "You know where you're going."

Side note: emotional trauma could lead to lots of soliloquies. Out loud. Thank God, I was alone more often than not, or I was certain people might consider me crazy.

Roughly an hour later, I was cursing my silly decision to try to be easy-going about my planning. Cell reception was total shit. My GPS seemed to truly be useless. To add to the mess, my SUV apparently had some kind of electrical malfunction because the speedometer kept blinking in and out. I presumed said electrical problem was the reason my GPS had abandoned me in my time of need.

"You're just looking for the name of the resort. You can find it. There will be a sign."

Yup, conversations with myself were the thing these days.

In most places, highways had signs—lots of signs—but Alaska kept it simple. There were mileage signs marking the distance to various towns, but I hadn't seen a single billboard. I recalled reading that Alaska had banned billboards upon its inception as a state. I supposed that was nice in theory, although I really, *really* wouldn't have minded one announcing my upcoming destination right about now.

The view was spectacular, and I'd seen several more moose as I'd traveled south. The one small problem, though, was that I was flying blind. The sun was starting its bow, and I was praying to reach my destination before it disappeared behind the mountains. Although it was August, the mountain peaks still had snow. Climate change was coming, but Alaska was hanging in there, at least at some elevations.

Walker Adventures was roughly twenty miles outside of one of Alaska's gems, Diamond Creek. Diamond Creek, the adjacent town near the resort, was where I intended to spend a month. That's right, an entire month in the wilderness. Me, Daphne Bell, doing something so wildly out of the ordinary that basically everyone I knew thought I was crazy.

I needed this almost as much as I needed air. My actual life, the one I left behind, was an epic mess and littered with regret, recrimination, and almost unbearable pain. Maybe, just maybe, I could piece myself together if I was far enough away.

"Oh! A sign! All you have to say is *resort*," I muttered to the green highway sign in question. "A little specificity never hurt anyone."

Fuck it. I took that left turn. The pavement stretched for a few miles and then transitioned. "Oh, hell," I murmured as the little blue SUV rumbled confidently over the gravel road. At least I made sure to rent a trusty vehicle with 4-wheel drive.

I kept on going, telling myself the same thing over and over again. *You'll find it, you're meant to be here, and it's all going to be okay.*

Considering I was thoroughly acquainted with just how *not* okay life could be, my faith in the universe was shaky at best.

Roughly forty-five minutes later, with one wheel mired deep in a mud puddle, I was staring at a bear. "Are you a brown bear or a grizzly bear?" I asked from the safety of my SUV as said bear ambled along the opposite side of the road, giving me nothing more than a cursory glance.

"Since when do roads not have shoulders?" I looked at my cell phone and glared at the no signal warning. "Fuck you."

The bear in question had caused me to swerve off the edge of the road, promptly dropping one rear wheel deep in the mud. I tapped my GPS button on the dashboard screen but got nothing. I didn't even know if I'd been speeding on the gravel road. My SUV seemed to be working, but the bells and whistles definitely weren't.

I heard a plane above and looked up at the sky through my windshield. Mind you, I didn't dare open my window in case the bear came over and ate my face.

"Oh, the plane's landing!"

The small plane descended in the sky and appeared to be landing not too awfully far away. But as the crow flew, or in this case literally as the plane flew, it could be as far as a few miles away. I didn't dare climb out and walk. Because: bears and God only knew what else.

My stomach growled, and I slapped my hand over it. I hadn't brought enough snacks. The resort promised a dinner tonight, and I thought for sure I would get there with hours to spare, so I'd eaten my last granola bar a few hours ago.

Leaning my head back against the seat, I took a deep breath and willed myself not to cry. I was going to be fine. If I had to walk, I would walk.

I heard a rustling sound, lifted my head, and screamed.

The bear was now right outside my car! Eating blueberries. I might not be a wildlife expert, but I knew blueberries when I saw them, and I'd run my car off the side of the road beside a small patch of them.

The bear lifted his head and eyed me dispassionately. I thought the bear was a he, although I had no idea why. While I was truly scared of the bear, he was a magnificent creature with gilded brown fur. He stared at me curiously for a moment after my scream, then he lowered his head and continued to eat. Somehow, it seemed ridiculous that this giant creature was nibbling—yes, nibbling—on blueberries.

I watched quietly, forgetting my predicament and forgetting the other disaster of my life as this massive bear that could probably kill me with nothing more than a gentle swat of its paw, meandered along eating blueberries. A few moments later, the bear disappeared into the trees, and I was alone again. A shaft of loneliness struck me so hard that it took my breath away.

"Daphne, you need a plan," I told myself sternly once I managed to take a breath.

I didn't know where to even begin with a plan, except hiking down this road and hoping it took me to the resort.

That spinning anxiety, a fucking whirling dervish, picked up in my chest again. I really didn't know what to do other than walk, and I could only pray I didn't have to walk too far.

Just when I was about to lose the battle with my tears, a truck appeared around the corner of the road ahead.

"Yay!" I literally lifted my fist in a cheer. I had no idea who this was, but I prayed they would stop.

Not thinking, I clambered out of the SUV and ran to the middle of the road, waving my arms like a crazy woman.

The black truck rolled to a stop. When I saw the man behind the steering wheel, I got a little intimidated. Friendly wasn't exactly the word that came to mind at his appearance.

The truck door opened, and he stepped out. My knees suddenly felt like liquid. Oh. My. God. His eyes flicked to my SUV, where it sat hanging off the side of the road with one wheel buried in the mud before his gaze landed on me. Good thing I had a few seconds to prepare myself.

When his glacial blue eyes locked with mine, an electric jolt sizzled through my body, setting every nerve ending alight with sparks. The man was tall and just plain built. His broad shoulders filled out his T-shirt. My eyes traveled down his arms, lean and muscled with a dusting of gold hair. He wore battered and faded jeans, which dipped at the waist when he hooked his thumb in a belt loop.

My eyes didn't miss the strip of tanned skin just below his T-shirt when he tugged down the waistband and revealed one side of a muscled V. I swallowed and dragged my eyes up. He had a jaw cut from granite and starkly angled cheekbones with an aristocratic nose. His lips were perfect. And then, as if to torture me, he had a dimple in the center of his chin.

I had clearly lost my mind because I felt my cheeks heat as my skin prickled all over.

"You must be Daphne," he said, his tone crisp.

All that came out of me in return was a gurgle. This man not only stole my breath but he also snatched away my ability to speak. This was new for me.

Chapter Two

FLYNN

The woman in front of me made some sort of gurgling sound and just stared at me. All things considered, I needed a moment, so I was grateful she gave me that.

Jesus fucking Christ. If this woman was trying to be more out of place, I didn't think she could swing it. Her auburn hair was in a braid, twisted neatly on top of her head with loose tendrils framing her face. She wore a skirt, a fucking skirt, on a gravel road in the middle of almost nowhere in Alaska. A pair of fitted black boots hugged her calves, and I had to will myself not to linger too long on her shapely legs. A silky blue blouse topped off her outfit. It was a freaking button-down blouse, and I had to work not to stare at the way the top button strained a little. She looked as though she would be right at home at some sort of sexy business meeting.

She gave off a princess vibe. There was no other way to describe it.

Her jade green eyes searched my face, and her cheeks flushed pink as we stared at each other.

"How do you know my name?" she finally asked, lifting her chin slightly and squaring her shoulders.

"Well, princess, I'm guessing you're the Daphne who has a reservation at the resort for a month."

The woman eyed me, her gaze uncertain and distrustful. When a light gust of wind blew a lock of her hair across her forehead, she released a puff of air, which expertly got it out of her eyes. "Fine. I am that Daphne. Is it necessary to call me princess?"

Dear God. This woman was something else. If she cleared five feet tall, that would be remarkable. She was short, petite, tidy, and gave off an uptight vibe. I didn't know what she was thinking when she signed up for a month at my family's adventure and expedition resort.

I was irritated. I was doubly irritated because my body seemed to think she was hot as all hell and then some. I couldn't fucking believe it, but when she spoke in that haughty, sharp tone and lifted her chin just a little bit more, my entire body tightened, and a shot of blood arrowed to my cock. What in the ever-loving hell was going on?

Daphne looked to the side, and I took a moment to absorb a few more details about her. My eyes dropped down to that button at the top of her blouse. I wanted to undo it. With my teeth.

Forcing my gaze upward, I traced along the angle of her jaw and the way her pert nose tipped up at the end. Her skin was rosy, like her lips, which were perfectly shaped. Just like a goddamn bow. Even worse, she had this little dimple on one side. She hadn't even smiled yet, but I could see the hint of it hiding there, waiting to peek out.

When she looked back toward me, her brow was knitted with worry. "I'm not sure why you're passing by, but I don't suppose you can help me with my, um, situation," she said, gesturing toward her little SUV.

"You're the reason I'm coming by. I saw your SUV from the air. That, and the bear."

"You could see me from the air?"

"Oh, yeah. It's a small plane, and I was coming down to land. Not too hard to see your bright blue SUV on the side of the road and a big brown bear grazing beside you."

"I really appreciate this. You don't happen to know who runs the resort, do you?"

"That's me."

"You're Flynn Walker?"

"At your service," I replied.

Daphne's eyes traveled up and down before landing on my face again. If I didn't know better, I'd think she was checking me out. But I knew better. No way was this uptight princess checking me out.

"Mind if I hop in your SUV?" I asked.

"I don't think you can drive it out," Daphne said as she stood planted in her boots and skirt in the middle of the road.

"Sure I can, princess. Give me those keys." As I approached her, she stood her ground, the pink tinge on her cheeks deepening. "I can get it out, no problem."

I kept on walking, and she spun quickly, hurrying to catch up with me. "Okay, the keys are in it. I'm sure you'll have to move the seat back."

Sliding my gaze sideways when I stopped to open the door, I said, "Oh, I'm sure about that. Mind if I try?"

"Be my guest," she said, gesturing with her hand as she stepped back. "If you can get me out of the mud, that would be wonderful."

The seat was practically kissing the steering wheel. I slid it back, climbed in, and started the SUV. After I closed the door, I rolled down the window. "You're going to need to step back. Mud's going to fly."

She crossed her arms and arched a brow. "All right then." She took several strides toward the other side of the road.

After starting the engine, I made sure the four-wheel drive was engaged. I tested it lightly to see if she had any traction on that one rear wheel. Not a damn bit. After a quick scan to get the lay of the vehicle's controls, I shifted it into differential gear. As soon as I felt it click into place, I gave the gas pedal a little pressure and felt the strong grind of the axle.

In another moment, the SUV bounced forward, and I heard Daphne squeal. I couldn't look her way just yet and eased the vehicle onto the road before I put it in park and cut the engine. When I climbed out, my mouth fell open. Daphne was covered in mud.

I bit back a smile. I didn't know how the hell that happened. From where she'd been standing, she should've been clear from the mud spray. When I met her eyes, a look of shock held for a beat before she threw her head back with a laugh.

Fuck me. The princess had a deep, throaty laugh when she let it loose.

I chuckled when she met my eyes again as her laughter slowed. "Oh, my God. I tried to be helpful and walked behind to give it a little push."

"You pushed?"

"No," she said, looking sheepish as she shook her head. She lifted a hand to smear some of the mud off her cheek. Not that it did anything to help. "I got back there right when whatever you did worked. The mud splattered all over me."

Daphne looked down. There was mud on her face, in her hair, and covering the entire front of her pretty blue blouse. There were splashes of mud on her skirt and her knees.

Hot damn, she looked sexy as hell covered in mud.

I was losing my mind. This inconvenient attraction to Daphne that came out of nowhere made absolutely no sense.

I tried to keep from laughing when she looked back up at me. She rolled her eyes, and that dimple made a sweet appearance when she smiled. "It's okay. You can laugh."

I chuckled softly. "I'm sorry. You just don't seem the type to get all muddy."

Her smile faded, and something flickered in her eyes, but she shuttered it quickly. "I aim to change that. Now, perhaps you can show me the way to the resort. If you didn't notice, my dashboard seems to be flickering in and out. My GPS is broken, and there's no cell phone reception here, so I wasn't even sure I was headed in the right direction."

"Well, gotta give it to you. You just kept on going."

She nodded, her chin lifting a bit again.

"Follow me then."

Chapter Three

DAPHNE

About ten minutes later, I stood beside Flynn and completely forgot I was covered in mud. "Oh, wow," I breathed reverently. "It's even prettier than the pictures."

Flynn angled his unsettling, sharp gaze to mine. This was the closest I'd gotten to him, and his eyes were like none I'd ever seen. The blue was encircled with a dark rim, almost as if an artist had shaded charcoal around the edges. "It's definitely nice," he commented.

"Nice?"

He shrugged. "Okay, beautiful."

The tiny hitch at one corner of his lips was enough to send my belly spinning in flips. Oh. My. God. If this man ever graced me with a full smile, I'd probably climb him like a freaking tree.

Heralded as one of Alaska's premier outdoor expedition resorts, Walker Adventures was a stone's throw from Diamond Creek, which I understood to be a town with plenty of restaurants and tourist attractions. But as I looked around, it was hard to imagine anything resembling civilization nearby. It truly felt as if we were in the middle of nowhere.

Spruce trees surrounded us. The resort, a massive timber-frame building, had dark stained wood siding with a blue steel roof covered almost entirely in solar panels. The building was the shape of an octagon with floor-to-ceiling windows on all sides and all three floors.

Flynn strode ahead of me and paused by the stairs, which led up to a wraparound deck. He'd insisted on getting my bags, hooking one over his shoulder and holding the other in his hand. "You ready to go in?"

I hadn't realized I'd frozen in place while my eyes absorbed the scenery. With trees to one side, the resort was set in the hills and offered an expansive view of the mountains on the other side. Those same bright fuchsia flowers I'd seen on my drive grew in clusters along the hillside. An ocean bay was visible in the distance with mountains on the far side.

"Yes!" I hurried to catch up to Flynn.

In my rush, the heel of my boot caught on a piece of gravel. I kicked it aside and stumbled slightly when I reached him. Flynn reached out to steady me, his free hand curling around my arm. His touch felt like a hot brand, and heat rushed through me.

"Have you forgotten you're covered in mud?" he asked, one side of his mouth tilting up in the slightest hint of a grin.

Oh, God. My body couldn't deal with any smiles from him, and I definitely couldn't handle him touching me. I swallowed as I tried to catch a breath. Although we were in rarefied mountain air, it suddenly seemed in short supply.

Looking down, I kept my sigh silent as I gathered myself. Dear God. I was an utter mess, literally and figuratively. When my eyes lifted to meet his again, and I saw the glimmer of warmth, I decided it couldn't be all that bad. Although I'd been born and raised to care deeply about appearances, I'd learned in the most brutal ways possible that appearances didn't matter. Not at all.

"I suppose I did forget about the mud," I offered with a brave smile.

"Come on in then."

Flynn gestured for me to climb the stairs in front of him. I figured the back of me looked better than the front, so I hurried up and waited by the doors.

"It's not locked," he said when he crested the top of the stairs.

"Oh," I squeaked before reaching to open the door. Considering he had my bags, the least I could do was get the door.

I stepped inside with Flynn following me. The entryway was tiled in slate gray. Rows of hooks on both walls flanked the door with grates on the floor.

Flynn must've seen my puzzlement as I eyed the grates curiously. "That's for during the winter. When people come in with snowy boots and gear, the water drains instead of pooling on the floor. Don't worry; it's not open to the outdoors. It's only about two inches under the floor and feeds into our drainage system."

"Oh, that's handy," I offered as I glanced up at him.

His gaze scanned my face, but I didn't know how to read his expression. He seemed quite skilled at keeping his thoughts hidden. Being an expert at that myself, I never held it against a person. Holding one's own counsel was important.

"Let me show you to your room," he said as he walked past me.

He led me through the tall archway into another

room. Just beyond the archway was a door on either side. The rest of the space was wide open. The hardwood floors gleamed under the sun shining through the windows. To one side, a small sectional sofa and a few chairs surrounded a soapstone woodstove. Another area had low bookshelves with more chairs, and then yet another area had a larger sectional couch with a television that came down from the ceiling. Without a single wall to divide the space, it somehow felt like three separate rooms due to the layout and flow.

I followed Flynn across the room to discover a pretty spiral staircase tucked in the corner. We crested the top stair, and he led me down the hallway before opening a door. The room had a view out over the field with the ocean glittering in the distance.

The clean, minimalist furnishings included a queen-size bed decorated in a fluffy cream-colored quilt with a nightstand on either side and a dresser across from the foot of the bed just beside the door where we stood. Flynn set my bags on the floor in front of the dresser and pointed at the door on the side of the room. "Shower's in there."

He turned, about to disappear through the doorway.

"Flynn."

He turned back, and this man was, simply put, *all* man—raw, rugged strength exuded from him. There was a hint of grace to the way he arched his brow. "Yeah?"

"The website said there were meals."

My words weren't quite a question, but Flynn nodded. "Yes. There are meals, princess."

I bit the insides of my cheeks to keep from reacting to that little nickname. There was no way he could've known I'd been given that very nickname when I was a little girl.

By the time I'd showered and changed into a pair of jeans with low-heeled boots and a mud-free cotton blouse, I could hear the murmur of voices and presumed another group of guests had arrived.

I didn't know why, but I felt a little anxious. I couldn't get Flynn's intense and striking eyes out of my mind. And every time he called me princess, a flash of irritation struck, followed immediately by a little kick in my pulse.

With a mental shake, I paused at the doorway, the feel of the doorknob cool under my palm before I turned it. On the heels of a deep breath, I squared my shoulders and walked down the hallway.

A tall, lanky young man came out of another door at an angle across the hallway. When he saw me, he cast me a quick grin. "Hello there."

I knew almost instantly that this young man had to be related to Flynn. He had the same amber hair kissed by the sun and those unique blue eyes with smoky edges.

"Hi," I managed politely.

He dipped his head in acknowledgment and gestured for me to walk ahead of him. "You must be Daphne," he said as we descended the spiral staircase.

"I am. How did you guess?"

"Well, the rest of the guests are here, and I haven't met a Daphne yet. I'm Grant," he offered when he stopped beside me at the base of the stairs. "Nice to meet you." His hand engulfed mine as he spoke. He was just as tall as Flynn but appeared younger.

"Nice to meet you as well," I said as I dropped his hand.

When I turned, I saw roughly ten people meandering about the common area downstairs.

"If you're hungry," Grant offered, "head on into the kitchen."

Following where he pointed, I went through one of the doorways flanking the archway into the main entrance. Trays of hors d'oeuvres lined the counter.

Although the space felt homey, it was clearly an industrial kitchen with massive appliances. Flynn was doing something on the stove at an island opposite the counter against the wall, and from the large rectangular table by the windows, I could see the hillside with the ocean in the distance.

Flynn glanced up when I entered. Something flashed briefly in his eyes as I approached, but it was gone before I could interpret it. "All cleaned up, I see," he said by way of greeting.

I felt the heat in my cheeks. I didn't even want to think about my reaction to Flynn. It seemed all I had to do was get close, and I got rattled.

"Anything to drink?" he asked.

"Sure."

"Beer or wine, or something else?"

"Wine, please. Red if you have it."

Flynn nodded and turned off the burner under the pan he'd been stirring. In another moment, he was filling a glass with dark red wine.

"So, you fly planes, fetch errant guests when they get stuck in the mud, and cook?" I teased politely.

Flynn turned to pass the glass of wine across the counter to me. Our fingers brushed, and a jolt of electricity sizzled up my arm. Little licks of fire chased over the surface of my skin in the wake of that subtle touch.

His hand dropped away, and I curled my fingers

around the wine glass to anchor me. His lips kicked up at one corner, and my belly was tickled by the butterflies that quickly amassed.

"I don't usually cook, but it's not because I can't. I'm more in charge of the flying and the fetching errant guests. Our chef quit last week, so we're short-handed. I'm covering until then."

"Oh." Brilliant answer. To mask my nervousness, I took a sip of wine, but it was too quick and too much. I sputtered and felt the cool wine strike my blouse as it splattered.

I met Flynn's eyes, which held a subtle gleam. "I seem to make a mess whenever I'm near you," I managed. My cheeks were flaming hot, and I wished I could will the heat away.

"Toss me that lashing strap, would you?" I called over to Elias.

The lashing strap came sailing through the air, and I caught the hook. Leaning into the storage area at the back of the plane, I tightened the strap and checked to make sure the hook was securely in place. Elias came around from the other side of the plane, resting his elbow on the wing as I straightened and closed the door to the rear compartment.

"Later this week, we have a group who booked a trip over to Katmai. You up for that?" I asked.

"Of course. What's the schedule until then?" he returned.

"Three flights tomorrow. How about you take one in the morning and afternoon, and I'll take the other one in the afternoon?"

He nodded immediately. Elias Lowe would live in the air if he could. He was one of my closest friends and had joined me here the year after I left the Air Force. We served together, but I'd left the military before he did because I needed to come home and take care of my siblings seven years ago.

I loved being in the air as much as he did, and it helped with the money we needed. People paid a ridiculous amount of money for flightseeing in Alaska and trips to remote travel locations. It wasn't cheap to fly, and the risks were high, but it was worth it. Aside from scrambling to get my family's outdoor expedition business in order when I came home, I had three younger siblings to take care of. So far, I'd managed to pay for college for Grant and Nora. My youngest sister, Cat, was still finishing high school.

Elias ran a hand through his shaggy dark blond hair and nodded. "You know I'll take every flight you throw my way."

"Oh, I know all right. It's just you can't be in two places at once."

"He'd like to think he could," a voice commented.

Elias rolled his brown eyes as he glanced over his shoulder. Tucker Harrison came into view as he stepped through the entrance into the plane hangar. "What the hell are you guys doing up this early?" he queried as he stopped on the other side of the plane's wing and rested both elbows on it.

"Working," Elias returned with a snort of a laugh.

"The more apt question would be what in the hell are you doing up so early?" I countered.

Tucker shrugged. "I know. Didn't sleep well last night. That new cook you hired is only mediocre at making coffee, by the way. Yours is better."

"Noted. So, you up for a couple of transport flights?"

Tucker nodded. "Of course. The fewer people I have to talk to, the better."

Elias slid his gaze sideways to Tucker. "We know that."

Tucker cracked a quick smile. He had a dry sense of humor with his friends, but he kept his friend circle small and tight. Like Elias, he served with me in the Air Force. When I'd heard from him three years ago, I invited him to come work with me, and he jumped on it. Tucker preferred to keep to himself, and Alaska was definitely a place that lent itself to that.

Patting the side of the small plane, I said, "You have mail and groceries for four villages. Might want to take a peek at the weather forecast, but I'm guessing it'll be a two-day loop to get everywhere you need."

"Works for me. If the plane's ready, I'll leave now," Tucker offered, running a hand through his rich brown curls.

"This baby's all loaded up," I said, glancing over my shoulder at the storage area to make sure I hadn't missed any boxes.

Tucker was already striding toward the small room that held various odds and ends, including gear. Not much later, he was steering the plane up into the clear sky.

Elias walked with me toward my truck in the parking area. "You taking the flight scheduled for this afternoon?" he asked as I pulled out my phone and scrolled through the schedule on the calendar.

"If you want it, it's yours. It's a family from New York. They were nice on the phone." Glancing at my screen again, I added, "They're supposed to be here in a half hour. Want to go grab some coffee first?"

"As if I would ever say no to coffee," he said dryly.

We were in town, the town being Diamond Creek. While I had a small gravel landing strip out near the resort, it was solely for personal use. We didn't do any official trips from there. The three plane hangars I owned here at the small airport in Diamond Creek were for my business's seven small planes. Every now and then, I marveled at that.

When I'd returned from the Air Force after my mom died, the finances were a mess. She'd started an expedition business with my stepfather—who'd been a fucking asshole, by the way—and the business never quite got off the ground. When I came home, I figured I'd work with what we had—a huge chunk of land close enough to Diamond Creek to make it valuable, a partially finished resort, and three planes. In the seven years since, I'd finished building the resort and seen a surprising uptick in business with our flightseeing.

Thank God for that because it made us good money. We made money at our resort as well, but the flights were *really* good money. I'd been able to expand in large part because I had enough pilots to fly the planes. In addition to Elias and Tucker, two more friends from the Air Force, Gabriel Hall and Diego Jackson, had also come out to work with me. Tucker's sister, Aubrey, would be joining us next year. Grant, my younger brother by five years, had finished his flight training last year. That gave me six pilots, including myself. My sister Nora was working on her flight training too.

I didn't trust many people, but these guys were like family to me. I trusted every single one of them implicitly.

"Damn, it's busy here," Elias said as I turned my truck into the parking area in front of Red Truck Coffee.

"It's always busy here," I returned. "Cammi's fast, though, so she'll have our coffee ready in no time."

We stepped up to the back of the line at the aptly named Red Truck Coffee. Housed in an old red truck that had been converted into a drive-by coffee shop and located right before the turn to the harbor docks in Diamond Creek, it did a brisk business from spring until the snow flew.

When we got to the front of the line, Cammi graced us with a wide smile. "Well, hey, boys. Flying the sunny skies today?" she asked, her blue eyes twinkling.

Cammi mostly ran this little coffee place on her own with occasional help during the busiest times of the year. You could almost always count on seeing her when you stopped for coffee.

I thumbed toward Elias. "He's flying this afternoon. I'm headed to do some repairs on one of our planes."

Cammi reached for one of her distinctive red paper coffee cups. "The usual for each of you?"

"I'll take an extra shot in mine today," I replied.

Elias gave a sharp nod. "Same."

Cammi started prepping our coffees. "Is neither one of you sleeping well?"

I shrugged. "It's just busy. Every fall, I tell myself it's going to slow down, but it never does."

"Not until after termination dust falls," Elias commented.

Cammi nodded in agreement. "Oh, yeah. The past few years, the tourist season seems to last longer and stay busier. It's like people are in a rush to see everything before all the glaciers melt."

She handed over one coffee, and I passed it to Elias, then fished some cash out of my wallet while she prepped mine. "When do you plan to close up shop for the winter?"

Cammi lifted one shoulder in a small shrug. "I never have a set day. I just wait until things slow down. Usually, that's late October or early November." She paused to fit a lid on my coffee. "Here you go." She slid the second coffee across the counter.

Handing her the cash, I looked toward Elias again. He was studiously quiet. It hadn't slipped my notice that he hardly talked whenever we stopped to get coffee here. But then, he wasn't the chattiest guy in general.

"Keep the change," I said as she began to open her cash drawer and count it out.

Cammi looked up. "That's a ridiculous amount of change, Flynn," she protested.

"And your coffee is ridiculously good. Right, Elias?" I nudged him with my elbow.

When he looked up, he simply nodded.

"Don't overdo it with the compliments, Elias," Cammi teased.

"Have a good one," I said, lifting my coffee cup in acknowledgment.

After we returned to my truck and were driving back toward the airport, I commented, "What gives with you whenever we're around Cammi?"

Elias shrugged when I slid my gaze sideways to him. "Nothing."

"Okay, whatever you say."

Elias took a swallow of his coffee. "It's not like she needs me to tell her the coffee is amazing every time we go there," he muttered after a moment.

I stayed silent and turned down the road that led to the runway. Diamond Creek's airport had two runways. One for the planes that came in from the airport in Anchorage and occasionally Juneau. Running parallel to that one was a shorter runway lined with the hangars for the small planes. A number of the small planes were owned privately, while just as many were owned by small businesses such as mine.

When I came back home after my mother died and stared down the debts she'd left behind, I needed a way to fix things fast. Not just for myself but also for my three younger siblings. My mother had already been struggling to stay afloat after my stepfather passed away. She'd never once complained, but it was clear she was skating by just to keep things above water. I'd never known my father and was the oldest of all four of us at thirty-two. Then came the three kids my mom had with my stepfather—Grant, Nora, and Cat. Grant was five years younger than me, Nora another two younger than him, and Cat was the surprise baby.

After returning home, I'd ramped up the expedition offerings at our small resort. I'd managed to pay off the debts left behind inside of seven years and put Grant and Nora through college. Cat was sixteen now, and the last one I needed to put through college.

To say my life was mostly work was an understatement. It was *all* work from sun-up until sundown. I was lucky that Alaska had longer days during the money season because every single hour counted.

Rolling to a stop, I glanced over at Elias. "So, you're all set for this afternoon?"

"I'll be back before sunset."

"See you later then. Fly safely."

Elias paused for a second with his hand hooked loosely on the door handle. "Always."

As I was driving out, a friend Trey Holden waved from his truck as I approached the stop sign onto the highway that would lead me out past Diamond Creek to home.

Stopping, I rolled my window down. "Hey, man, what's up?" I asked, leaning my elbow on the window.

"Got something for you to think about," Trey began. "I'm planning to sell my plane and the business that goes with it."

"Really?" I asked, my mind immediately skimming through the numbers in the ever-present balance sheet in my brain.

Trey was a fellow pilot who ran a much smaller version of what we did. It was just him and his one plane and very part-time. Additionally, he was an attorney, which I figured kept him plenty busy.

Trey nodded. "Yeah. Emma's pregnant again." A wide smile broke across his face.

"Congratulations! I know you've been hoping for another one. When's the baby due?"

"Six months."

"That's awesome. I'm seriously happy for you. I'm guessing you'd like to work a little less?"

"You got it. And stay closer to home. I have more business than I know what to do with as it is. Honestly, if I could just fill in and take flights for your business in a pinch, I would love it. That would scratch my flying itch, and I wouldn't need to worry about the business end of things. I'm gonna finish out the season because I have too many booked, but you let me know come winter what you wanna do. I'd rather sell to you than anyone else."

"Might be able to get more money than I can give you. Just being honest," I offered.

Trey shrugged. "Maybe. But I trust you, and I like you. So, there's that. I gotta run, though. I already have customers waiting."

We waved, and I drove off, seriously considering Trey's offer. For one, that would give me another plane and hangar. Two, I immediately had a backup pilot, and Trey was as solid as they came. Three, more money.

Chapter Five

DAPHNE

Standing on the beach, I breathed in the crisp, briny air while soaking in the view. The icy cold waters of Kachemak Bay lapped at my feet as small waves broke along the shoreline. My eyes landed on a deep red piece of rock, and I leaned over to lift it out of the cold water. It was light, and I guessed it was probably a piece of hardened lava.

Drying it on my jeans, I tucked it into my pocket and continued to walk along the shore. Nora had given me directions to this trail when I told her I wanted to go for a walk on the beach. She assured me it was a well-traveled trail, and I didn't need to worry about too much wildlife. She had cautioned, "There's always some wildlife, but I wouldn't send you there if I thought you were gonna run into some brown bears. Moose are everywhere. Just make a bunch of noise and yell at them if necessary."

Because this entire trip was about me trying new things, I'd hoped she didn't see the anxiety I felt inside. I'd nodded and driven into town. I'd been in Alaska for almost five days now. So far, every day had brought something new, starting with the hike planned by Flynn's younger brother, Grant. Another day took me out on the water in a boat to fish, and I'd taken several hikes near the resort itself.

I was definitely escaping, but I hadn't had much time to myself. On day three, Flynn had offered to look at the electrical problems with my rented SUV and magically fixed it. Although I doubted it was magic. It just seemed like it to me because I knew nothing about cars and wiring.

When I offered to pay him something, he turned his glacial blue gaze on me and shook his head, dismissing me. I was pretty sure he could hardly stand me. As for me, well, it felt as if a switch flicked on in my body when I was near him. My signals went haywire, and I couldn't think. He made me feel hot; a kind of hot I'd never encountered. Every time I was around him, my heart thumped so hard it felt as if it were trying to break free from my chest. And here I thought myself well beyond desire and perfectly content with that state of affairs.

Flynn had me horny. That's right, horny. Meanwhile, he could barely look at me for more than a few seconds. He still called me princess, which drove me just crazy enough that I was determined not to let it show.

As I walked, occasionally kicking stones with the toe of my boot, Brandon's face flashed in my thoughts. It had been a year since he died—to the day, in fact— yet I could still remember his round blue eyes and his silly smile. He was the goofiest little boy—*was* being the operative word.

I was strangely relieved to reach this day and realize I could still breathe and move. Because the loss of my son literally took my breath away at times and left me staggering.

When a loss that brutal is experienced, several things happen inside. For one, I'd become an absolute master of faking it to make it. There were days when I couldn't do that, but other days when I learned to put one foot in front of the other and go through the motions of life while trying not to look like I was completely out of my mind with grief. Over time, the brutally sharp pain did start to fade and lessen.

I knew some people worried they would forget their child's face. Sometimes I wished I could, if only to ease the pain of remembering. I clung to those memories in my mind, like opening a scrapbook and flipping through all of my favorites.

There was a splash in the water, and I glanced out, seeing nothing at first. My eyes skimmed up to the mountains across the water. Cat told me the other day about termination dust. At sixteen, Flynn's younger sister was filled with information and offered it freely. She loved to talk.

Apparently, the first snow that coated the tops of the mountains was called termination dust. Cat told me sometimes it came as early as October or November, but we weren't there yet. Termination dust or not, the mountains were spectacular. The sun glinted on the ruffled surface of the water as I stared out over it.

A sleek head appeared out of the water, maybe fifteen feet from the shore. It was a seal, and my heart gave a beat of wonder. It stared at me curiously, and I could see its liquid dark eyes. After a moment, it dove underwater before surfacing. I smiled, thinking Brandon would've loved to have seen a seal.

There it went. It was like a knife slicing through

my lungs and heart at once. The pain was sharp, and my eyes stung from it.

I was used to it now. Once I could breathe again, I resumed walking. Glancing down at my watch, I realized I'd been walking along the beach for an hour, so I figured I should probably turn back.

Retracing my steps, I found the narrow path through the tall grasses just beyond the rocky beach. The landscape transitioned quickly into a boreal forest with spruce trees towering tall, and the golden leaves from the birch trees fluttered through the air, covering the path under my feet, almost in welcome.

As I rounded a corner, not too far from where my vehicle was parked, I heard a huffing sound. Freezing in place, I looked around to see a giant moose. Cat had offered up that they were nearsighted just yesterday, yet even if the moose in question couldn't see me, it was definitely aware of my presence. Facing me, he pawed the ground.

I swore silently, "Oh, fuck."

As Nora had said, though, the moose kept his distance and didn't appear to be approaching me. Although the most direct route for me was to walk ahead, that was where the moose was. Looking to my left, I walked into the trees, glancing back to see that he wasn't following me. I figured I would detour far enough away and loop back.

For a few minutes, all was well as I picked my way through the trees. Then I hooked a right to bring me back in the correct direction. Another minute later, I was facing a steep rocky cliff. It was maybe only ten feet, but it wasn't the nice level path the moose was blocking.

"Daphne, just climb on up. You've got this," I whispered to myself.

I *did* have it. Of course, I managed to scrape my elbow and tear my jeans, but whatever. I thought I was doing great until I slipped in a muddy patch after I made it to the top of the cliff and landed in a bush, the meanest bush I'd ever encountered in my life with sharp spikes on thick branches. It didn't draw blood, but it hurt like hell.

With my breath hissing, I stumbled back to my feet and was relieved that I could see the glint of my blue SUV through the trees. I only hoped my moose friend hadn't meandered farther up the trail to the parking area. If so, I was screwed.

Blessedly, there was no sign of the moose, and I was on my way back to Walker Adventures within a few minutes. Cat had actually entered the official map address in my GPS for me.

"So, you can't ever forget how to get back," she'd said this morning with a sly grin.

I wanted to stop in Diamond Creek and maybe get some coffee or food at a restaurant, but my scraped elbow hurt, and I was dirty. The town was cute with brightly painted signs along the main street and tourists everywhere. Although autumn was approaching in a few weeks, and the days were getting cool and the nights downright chilly, it didn't seem to slow down the visitors.

Roughly twenty minutes later, I was driving past the very spot where I'd seen the bear when my tire got stuck in the mud. I couldn't help but smile. Flynn must've thought I was crazy. I'd definitely been overdressed.

Not that I brought too many nice clothes on this trip, but online, the resort was billed as high-end. It certainly wasn't cheap, and the food was pretty good. I could be a snob about food. Not because I expected it to be amazing, but because I'd once run my own bakery and café. I loved, absolutely *loved*, to cook and bake.

I swatted away a memory that briefly flickered in my mind—one of Brandon while he stood on a stool I'd gotten for him as he helped me make cookies.

At least this trip to Alaska provided such a departure from my life that I didn't dwell too much on things. I needed the distance, and I needed the space.

My heart gave a little jump when I turned the corner and the small resort came into view. The building was beautiful, and the views were utterly breathtaking. I still felt like a child in a candy shop, in awe of the novelty and breathtaking beauty.

I parked and sighed as I looked down at the mud on one of my knees and the scrape on my elbow. Although I'd yet to repeat my first day when I got mud everywhere, I was trying not to look like too much of a fool around Flynn.

I told myself it didn't matter what he thought anyway. Our worlds were so far apart that my body's insane reaction to him was going to fade. It had to.

Moments later, I was reaching for the handle on the door that led into the main entrance when it swung open. My pulse took off like a rocket at the sight of Flynn standing there. As usual, he wore a faded pair of jeans and a long-sleeve T-shirt. If there was such a thing as a uniform out here, this was definitely his.

The T-shirt did an utterly poor job of masking his fit and scrumptious body. His glacial blue eyes swept me up and down. He surprised me when his gaze narrowed in concern.

"What happened?" he asked.

Before I could reply, he was tugging me through

the door. "Let's get you some first aid and get you cleaned up."

"I'm fine," I said hurriedly. I didn't like to need anything from anyone.

I certainly didn't want to impose on Flynn. Spending too much time near him generally left me feeling as if I was knocked off my axis and stumbling for my balance. And hot, usually hot all over. Because he was hot, *way* too hot for my sanity.

Flynn ignored me. He pulled me through a door at the back of the kitchen, which led to an entirely private section of the resort. We walked through what appeared to be a living room and into a large bathroom where Flynn began rummaging through the cabinet. Next thing I knew, he had me by the sink and was cleaning off my elbow.

"Tell me if it stings," he said.

I highly doubted I would even notice if it did. My breath was shallow, my heart was banging around inside my chest, and my belly was filled with butterflies.

Flynn was right here, every strong and sexy inch of him. His touch was gentle and light, and my eyes were mesmerized by his hands. He had big hands with long fingers, almost elegant. Rugged as he was, he had a confident grace to the way he moved.

After he neatly cleaned up my elbow and put a bandage over it, he looked down at my leg with mud smeared from my knee upward and the ragged tear on my jeans. "I think you're going to need to change for me to check on that."

Although Flynn had addled my thoughts and stolen all of my breath, it seemed I hadn't completely lost my mind. "It's okay," I said, breathlessly enough that I was embarrassed. "I can take care of it."

His eyes lifted to mine. Sweet Jesus. His gaze was intense. "Did you bump into some devil's club?"

"Huh?" I asked brilliantly.

He gestured toward the punctures in the side of my jeans where I'd landed on that mean bush.

"Oh, is that what that awful bush is called? Devil's club?"

Flynn's lips kicked up slightly at one corner. "Yeah, princess. If it was a low bush with thick stalks and nasty thorns, it was devil's club."

"Well, it certainly hurt. If you don't mind, I'll clean my knee up and meet you outside. Or I can just take some of the first-aid stuff and take care of it in my room." I needed to get myself out of Flynn's close presence before I did something stupid.

For a moment, he stood right where he was, and I sensed his indecision. He said nothing, though, and stepped back. The sound of the door shutting behind him was a loud click in the tiled bathroom.

Relieved to be alone again, because I could barely stand to be that close to Flynn, I took a moment to orient myself. This bathroom had a large oval-shaped tub in one corner and a really sweet shower with a rain shower faucet and other fixtures on the walls. Right about now, I could've seriously used a shower, so I imagined it would be heaven.

With a mental shake, I shimmied out of my jeans and cleaned up my knee. I hadn't even broken the skin where I'd landed. It was just red and irritated. I inspected the marks from the devil's club. There were only three, and they looked innocuous enough, but they ached.

After slipping my jeans back on, I returned every-thing to the first-aid kit and stepped out of the bath-room. Flynn was waiting by the windows, looking out over the mountains. His hands were in his pockets, and he looked pensive.

I cleared my throat. He turned quickly, his eyes sweeping over me. Having Flynn's focus on me was unsettling. His gaze felt like a beam of fire on my body. I didn't think that was what *he* intended, but my body definitely had a mind of its own when it came to Flynn.

"You okay?"

"Of course. Thank you for the first aid." Uncertain what to do, I twisted my fingers together. "Um, I'll go then."

Flynn continued as if I hadn't said anything. "Where the devil's club got you will be sore, but that's it. Ibuprofen helps. If you don't have any, we have some."

"Okay. Thank you."

At that, Flynn strode across the room, swiftly closing the distance between us. "Are you planning to take any flightseeing trips?"

He kept walking past me, so I simply turned and followed him. "I'd like to. I just, well, I've never been on a plane that small."

Flynn was opening the door, and he stopped to look back at me. His gaze was inscrutable, but then it almost always was. "You'll like it. It's the best way to get a good view. The family that arrived today scheduled one soon. There should be an extra seat if you want to tag along."

"Geez, Flynn, I'd almost think you were trying to be nice."

Chapter Six

FLYNN

I almost laughed at that. Every now and then, I saw sparks of the woman I sensed was behind the smoke screen Daphne created. She was so buttoned-up that it was obvious she was carrying something inside. I had no idea what and reminded myself almost daily that it was none of my damn business.

I bit back my smile. "I can be nice, princess. Now come on, you don't want to miss dinner."

Daphne lifted her chin a little as she walked past me, and I resisted the urge to reach out and tap her cute ass. I was startled at how much I had to clench my hands. Daphne was going to drive me insane before the end of her trip. I couldn't help but wonder where she got the money to spend a month in Alaska. And by herself, no less.

The questions just kept coming for me with Daphne. As it was, I didn't dare ask a single one. My curiosity about Daphne was entirely out of the ordinary. I didn't have time for a woman, much less one who brought out every crazy instinct in me. Someone, or something, had hurt her badly. I wanted to know who or what.

I knew pain when I saw it because I knew it far too well myself. Every now and then, I saw the shadows in her eyes, and I saw how she clamped her guard down. I physically shook my head to chase my curiosity away.

Roughly an hour later, I was relieved that we were busy with guests. The resort could host up to thirty people at a time, and we were completely booked. We'd been completely booked all of this season and the one prior. The flight business had taken off sooner. Now that this place was getting busier, my schedule was more insane than it had ever been.

I was accustomed to being busy. When I was in the Air Force, my entire days were mapped out. I was busy from sun-up to sundown then and even during the night sometimes, but my schedule ran like a clock. Everything had a system and a structure, even emergencies.

Flying in Alaska is considered one of the riskiest occupations because the weather is unpredictable, as is the landscape. There are too many contingencies to plan around. I'd figured the flying would be my challenge, and it was. It kept me on my toes all the time.

Yet what I'd thought would be the easier part of running this fledgling expedition resort wasn't turning out to be easier. Guests were unpredictable, and managing the staff I needed to make it work was even more challenging.

Striding into the kitchen, I looked around for the woman I'd just hired last week, but Tonya was nowhere to be found. Crossing the room, I poked my head into the large pantry, and I found her there, texting on her phone.

"Tonya?" I called from the doorway.

She looked up, appearing entirely unconcerned that I just discovered her wasting time in the pantry. "Yeah?"

"What's the status of dinner?"

Annoyance flashed in her eyes. Her shoulder was resting against the pantry shelves, and she didn't even move.

I was so fucking done with this. I wanted to fire her on the spot, but for now, she was my help. "Ever hear of cooking?" I pressed.

Oh, great. Now she looked hurt.

"I'll be right there, Flynn," she muttered. "I just came in here to get some ingredients."

On my way out of the pantry, my eyes immediately landed on Daphne. She was at the long table in the front area of this room, talking with Cat.

When I saw the curve of her smile and the dimple in her cheek peek out, I felt a tug low in my gut. In response, I immediately stalked out of the kitchen.

Just as I was pushing through the doors into the main room, Gabriel and Diego almost collided with me as they came through in the opposite direction. Diego hitched his brows. "Where are you running off to?"

"Just grabbing something from my truck," I practically barked in return.

Anger and annoyance seemed to be the flipside to my desire for Daphne. She had me unsettled, shaking the grip I had on my life. I had priorities, and a sexy, out of place princess torturing me just for existing wasn't one of them.

She's not as much princess as you think, a voice taunted in my thoughts.

Shut the fuck up.

She wasn't, though. Oh, she definitely had that princess vibe. Even when she was dressed down, she was perfectly put together. But she was pretty down to earth. She didn't expect anyone to wait on her. If anything, she resisted asking for help. When I'd offered to look at the electrical problem on her rental, she chewed on her bottom lip—driving me wild in the process for a solid minute—before she finally said yes.

And here I was, thinking about Daphne. Again. I pointlessly walked out to my truck and pretended I was looking for something in the glove compartment. I was behaving like an idiot just so I could make it seem like I'd actually left the kitchen for some reason other than avoiding Daphne.

Returning, I was relieved to find Gabriel and Diego seated at the island in the kitchen. Nora had joined Cat and Daphne, along with a few of the other guests at the table. Tonya was blessedly working.

Passing the guys, I asked, "Beer? I have some fresh brew from Diamond Creek Brewery."

"Always," Diego replied with a quick grin while Gabriel nodded.

After I fetched the growler I'd gotten from the local brewery, I snagged three pint glasses and tugged a stool to the corner of the island. I told myself it wasn't because I could surreptitiously take peeks at Daphne.

She was so fucking sexy, though. She had changed after cleaning up the scrape on her knee into a fitted cotton T-shirt with a scoop neck that made me want to trace my tongue over the curve of her breasts that barely rose above the top. She'd paired that with jeans.

Daphne was not my type. She was always put together, even in just jeans and a T-shirt. She was petite and tidy with her luscious breasts and beyond tempting if only because the rest of her was slim.

"Yeah, I know," Gabriel's voice reached my ears.

Looking his way, I asked, "You know what?"

"You're staring at Daphne again," Diego offered with a sly grin.

"No, I'm not," I lied.

"Okay, you're not," Gabriel said affably.

With his auburn hair and bright blue eyes, Gabriel tended to be a draw for single women who were visiting the resort and those crowding Diamond Creek, when he went to town for a little night fun.

Gabriel was one of my closest friends, and I trusted him with my life. It was a fact he'd actually saved mine once. I'd returned the favor another time in a dicey rescue mission. When it came to women, Gabriel liked playing the field and had probably never spent more than one night with any particular woman.

His eyes narrowed in calculation after my comment. "Well, if you're not chasing after her, maybe I will."

Over my dead body. I took a gulp of my beer and leveled him with a look. "Don't you dare. Maybe she's not for me, but she's definitely not here for your fun."

"All right, you owe me a hundred bucks," Diego said.

"I do?" I countered.

"No, Gabriel. He bet me that if he said that to you, you'd tell him he couldn't. I didn't think you had the nerve. Guess I was wrong."

Gabriel chuckled. "Don't worry, man. None of us here would hit on Daphne. It's obvious you've got a thing for her."

I rolled my eyes and took another swallow of my beer. "Fuck off."

"This is not specific to Daphne, although she does have the honor of being the first woman I've seen you even kind of interested in, but you could loosen up. Life doesn't have to be all work and so freaking serious," Diego offered.

"You guys know I've still got to scrounge up the money to put Cat through college. That means work and a lot of it." I shifted my shoulders, annoyed at how defensive I felt.

"And you're making plenty," Gabriel said. "Ran into Trey Holden, by the way. He mentioned he's giving you first dibs when he puts his business up for sale after the end of the season. Think you'd be smart to take him up on it."

"Agreed. I'm gonna talk to the bank when I find the time. I don't have the cash myself. I put too much toward expanding the resort and the flight schedule as we have it."

"You've done a damn good job," Diego said with a firm nod.

At that moment, Cat, sixteen years old and with enough attitude to drive me insane, stopped beside us. "Can I go out with Jonathon tomorrow in his boat?" she said, referring to her new boyfriend. I didn't even know if he was actually her boyfriend, but I didn't know what else to call him in my mind.

"No, just no." Cat opened her mouth to argue, but I shook my head again. "I'm not saying yes to you going out on the bay with anyone who isn't an adult."

"He's been out in boats a lot," Cat muttered.

"He's sixteen. He can only have so much experience. The weather can turn on a dime out there. I'm just not comfortable with it."

"What if I took someone with me?" she countered.

I shook my head again. "Not unless it's an adult I can talk with."

"Flynn, you say no to everything."

I took a gulp of my beer for some fortitude. "Cat, I definitely don't say no to everything. Please don't argue like this. I'm not going to change my mind."

Cat sighed, sounding all put upon. "I don't see why it's a big deal. It's not like we're going to make out on the boat."

"I was a teenage guy once. Trust me, Jonathon is hoping otherwise," I muttered.

Cat glared at me. Diego was biting the insides of his cheeks to keep from laughing. Gabriel had turned away, although I could see his shoulders shaking.

"Fine. Can I go with Daphne to Diamond Creek tomorrow?" Cat asked.

"Is all your homework done?"

Tomorrow was Saturday, but Cat was freaking smart as hell and taking college courses now through a high school program to get ahead for when she eventually started college.

Cat nodded quickly. "Of course." Although she may try to push my limits on just about everything else, I never doubted her when she answered on her school status. She took school seriously and busted her butt.

"Then, yes. But I need to check with Daphne first."

Cat rolled her eyes but then dipped her chin in acknowledgment. "Fine." She spun away, skipping out of the dining area.

"Be right back," I said as I stood and crossed the room to approach Daphne.

It didn't help matters that every time I got near Daphne, my body revved its engine like the start of a race. Daphne had just turned away from whomever she was speaking with and was standing by the windows.

Stopping beside her, I looked out to see clouds burgeoning in the sky over the bay. They hadn't blotted out the setting sun yet, but it was close. Taking a breath, I braced myself to look at Daphne. When I turned, she was still looking forward.

God, she was beautiful. Her auburn hair was down now, falling halfway down her back. It had gold highlights in it, almost as if she'd caught a little bit of sunshine in the locks. Her nose turned up at the end, and I wanted to kiss her pretty pink lips. Okay, I was definitely losing my mind.

"So, Cat asked me if she could go to Diamond Creek with you tomorrow. I'm assuming she asked you first," I began.

Daphne turned toward me then. For a split second, the heat blasted me, sizzling up my spine. Her tongue darted out, and she licked her lips.

"She did. I'd love to take her since she knows her way around. I told her she had to ask you, though," Daphne said.

"It's fine. Fair warning, she'll talk your head off."

Daphne's smile unfurled slowly, and it was like a punch to my gut. My balls tightened. "I can handle it. Cat's delightful. If you didn't know, she adores you. She brags about you almost every time I talk to her."

I laughed softly. "Is that so? Well, good thing, because she's stuck with me for a few more years."

I saw the questions swirling in Daphne's eyes. It's just I didn't feel like answering them. Instead, I was an ass. "Do me a favor, though, don't get stuck on the side of the road."

Chapter Seven

DAPHNE

My cell phone vibrated on the dresser in my room at the resort. It was only six a.m. here, but that meant it was noon back in Atlanta. I didn't expect many calls, so I assumed it was someone from home.

Despite the location, there was good reception here because they had a cell tower on a ridge nearby. Lifting my phone from the dresser, I glanced at the screen and saw my mother's name flash.

The phone vibrated in my hand two more times before I swiped my thumb across the screen and brought the phone to my ear. "Hey, Mom."

"Daphne! How are you, dear?"

My mother sounded friendly and had injected an extra dose of cheer into her tone. I knew better than to let my guard down. Tension coiled in my gut.

"I'm fine, Mom. How are you?"

"Well, I've been wondering when you were going to give up and come home. Alaska is not exactly your style."

I gritted my teeth and curled my free arm around

my waist as I strode to look out the windows. I didn't really know what my style was.

"I'm enjoying it here." My voice came out smoothly despite the tightness in my chest and the icy ball of dread in my stomach. "How are you?" I repeated.

"Not well. Not well at all. We need you here. Your father needs your help to smooth things over with some of our partnerships."

"Mom, when I come home, I'm not re-opening the restaurant. And I'm definitely not working in the business anymore."

"Daphne," my mother began, her tone going exactly where I predicted it would go—sharp and judgmental. "I know you're devastated about Brandon's death."

My breath seized in my lungs. My heart felt as if hundreds of tiny cracks were spreading, and it might shatter into pieces. I stayed silent, and after another moment, my breath came back. My mother's voice picked back up over the rushing sound in my ears.

"I know what Pete did feels inexcusable, but nothing is unforgivable. We all make compromises every day of our lives. Chin up and come back home."

"No," I said flatly, my voice coming out stronger than I expected. "I don't know what I'm going to do, but I absolutely refuse to help smooth over the situation. Pete cheated on me with someone I thought was my friend at an absolutely horrible time. This isn't just about forgiveness. I'm working on forgiveness, but forgiveness doesn't mean I have to be friends with anyone again. It certainly doesn't mean I need to make nice and work with people I will never trust in my life. Forgiveness is just about finding peace for myself."

"Daphne, your father needs you. Pete is indispensable in this business, but so are you. He needs you both, and he needs it to work."

God, my mother was freaking amazing. She just couldn't let herself consider how I might be doing. She wanted *me* to be the one to gloss this over.

"Mom, it's not happening. Go ahead and cut me off. I don't need anything from you. I know it infuriates you, but Gram left me everything." I was the only grandchild on my father's side. My grandmother was one of the few people I'd been able to turn to after my life blew up. I'd lost her too, but she'd made sure I could do whatever I wanted by leaving me everything she had. "I'll be fine on my own. The fact that you keep asking me to do this only drives me further away from you and Dad. Now, I'm getting off the phone. Goodbye."

I didn't hear what my mother said next because I just hung up the phone. My hand was shaking so hard as I lowered the phone. I was relieved the bed was right beside me because I lost my grip, and my phone fell on the mattress.

I found out the month before my little boy died that my ex, Pete, had been having an affair with a close friend for over a year. My close friend who worked with me. My ex was my father's second in command at his high-end investment and property management business in Atlanta. Pete and I were the golden couple or something like that. Our families had shared business interests, and it was supposed to be wonderful that we fell in love and got married. Wonderful, my ass. It turned out to be built on sand.

I'd once been in the thick of it all. I'd been raised to be polite and just do what my family needed. I'd never questioned whether I'd work for my father. My parents weren't warm and fuzzy, but I'd mistakenly believed they would put my interests first when every-thing blew up. Ha.

Not at all. Everyone had told me to make nice with Pete, who'd been fucking my friend while our son was dying.

I'd been the primary point of contact for publicity within my family's business. It had been my job to make things look good and put the best spin on any situation. I couldn't do that anymore, not when it meant selling out myself.

I took several deep breaths as I paced back and forth in front of the windows. I needed to discharge the toxic energy stirred up by my mother's call. I didn't know where I was going after this trip, but I had come to one clear-eyed conclusion since I'd arrived in Alaska.

I wasn't returning to Atlanta to live. There was nothing to hold me there. There were too many strings trying to tie me to things I needed to break away from. My little boy's absence was a gaping hole in my life, and a wound in my heart I didn't think would ever stop bleeding. The only thing I missed from Atlanta was my restaurant.

My parents had referred to it as my "vanity" project. I loved to cook and bake. Without borrowing a single penny from my parents, I'd taken out a loan on my own and opened it. I'd cut back my hours at the family business to make it work. Against the doubts of my parents, my small bakery and café had taken off. I was sensible enough to know a bit of that was luck. Because a bit of every success involved the whimsy of timing and luck.

When Brandon was diagnosed with a rare form of brain cancer, I'd done the research and knew his chances of survival were incredibly poor. At the height of its success, I'd closed my restaurant to spend more time with my son. I didn't want to miss a minute of the time I could have with him. Those months felt like stolen time. I'd tried to grab the vagaries of fate and yank time to a stop.

I didn't realize I was crying until I felt a hot tear roll down my cheek, cooling as it moved over my skin. I dragged my sleeve across my cheeks and pondered letting myself cry for hours.

I looked out the windows, across the field of fading pink flowers that I now knew to be fireweed. My eyes lifted over the tops of the spruce trees to the sparkling water of the ocean bay in the distance. I came here for a change of pace, but more than that, I'd come to Alaska to try to figure out what I wanted. I'd needed the span of the continent between my family and me.

Maybe I didn't have the answer I sought yet, but I knew I didn't want to sit in this room and cry. I grabbed my fleece jacket and hurried out into the hallway. After I had breakfast, I figured I would take advantage of Cat's request to go with me to Diamond Creek. She'd talk my ear off, and that was exactly what I needed.

Chapter Eight

FLYNN

Three weeks after Daphne's arrival

"Daphne!" I called.

She turned, and her auburn hair lifted in the breeze. I'd become accustomed to the low hum of electricity that ran through my body like a repeating circuit around her even though I willfully ignored it.

"Yes?" She approached me where I was standing beside my small plane.

In the three weeks Daphne had been here, she stopped wearing blouses and nice boots but somehow still looked like a princess. Today, she wore a pair of jeans that fit like a glove, molding to her toned thighs before disappearing into a pair of hot pink rubber boots with black polka dots. Atop that, she wore a fitted T-shirt that had *Kickass Woman* emblazoned in pink glitter directly over her breasts. God help me.

"Mind sitting on the wing?" I asked.

"Excuse me?" she countered in a crisp yet incredulous tone.

"Yeah, I need a little weight to lower the back of the plane. I think you're the perfect size."

Daphne's mouth fell open before she snapped it shut quickly. "I don't even know how to interpret that comment."

"Just being practical, princess."

She never said a word to me about it, but I knew it annoyed her when I called her that. I just couldn't resist getting under her skin. Perhaps it was because she was under my skin *all* the fucking time, in *all* the wrong ways. Maybe I should've wondered about that, but I tried to avoid thinking too much about Daphne. She invaded my senses so thoroughly, and avoidance was my only escape.

"Happy to help. I just don't think I can climb up there," she said as she eyed the plane wing in question.

"Come here," I replied, gesturing with a hand.

When she stepped closer, I rested my hands at her waist. Mistake. Big mistake. I'd spent three full weeks studiously avoiding getting too close to Daphne. Touching her was like touching a live wire as far as my senses were concerned. Every nerve ending sparked and vibrated to her frequency.

I had no choice but to forge ahead even though I could feel the heat of her skin through her thin cotton T-shirt. I had to clear my throat to speak. "Ready?" I asked, my voice coming out husky.

Daphne's jade eyes held mine, darkening as we stared at each other. For one completely insane second, I almost kissed her.

What snapped me out of it was when she lifted her chin slightly. She did that whenever she was uncertain about something. Those moments had become less frequent in the time she'd been here. Although she hadn't shared much, I could've guessed she was a city girl through and through.

"Ready," she whispered. The hitch in that single word sent a tendril of silk around my heart. Sweet hell. It was bad enough to want Daphne. I did *not* need to *feel* something for her.

I lifted her quickly, sliding her hips on the plane wing. As I knew it would, the plane dipped down in the back, lowering the back door to make it easier for me to help an elderly passenger in.

Against every ounce of common sense I had, my hands stayed right where they were, curled around her hips. I could feel the soft give of her flesh under my grip. When I looked up, I saw the rapid flutter of her pulse in her neck. My mouth watered. That was how much I wanted to lean forward and taste her skin.

I stepped back abruptly. "Excellent."

After I helped the elderly woman who'd come to our resort with her adult daughter and son-in-law into the plane and the other two passengers, I turned to help Daphne down off the wing.

I didn't know if it was better or worse that I tried to steel myself for the jolt of lust I knew would hit me the moment I placed my hands on Daphne again.

Worse, definitely worse. Because my effort was useless, and it only served to remind me just how little control I had when it came to Daphne.

The moment I set my hands on her hips, her scent drifted to me. For some reason, a hint of sugar clung to her. I'd never thought of anyone as delicious, but that was exactly how I knew Daphne would taste. In more ways than one.

I lifted her swiftly, practically jumping back once her feet were level on the gravel. "You get the view today," I said as I gestured toward the front of the plane.

"I do?" Her pretty green eyes lit up, and it felt as if another tendril of silk spun around my heart.

I might be cynical, and I might be too damn busy to deal with a woman who was so clearly out of her element, but I loved how expressive Daphne was. Sometime last week, a mama moose and a pair of triplet calves were meandering through the field in front of the resort, and Daphne's entire face had been awash in wonder and awe.

In an effort to curb my reaction to her, my response came out sharp. "Sure do."

Rounding the front of my small plane, I opened the door and gestured for her to climb in. Fuck me. As she climbed in, I had a perfect view of her heart-shaped ass. It sent another bolt of need slamming through me.

I was pretty sure she thought I was a fucking asshole since I was easily annoyed and cranky whenever I was around her. All things considered, she was probably right. I was relieved she'd be gone from the resort in another week or so, and I could get back to being normal, as my little sister had pointed out the other day.

Actually, what Cat asked was, "What the hell is wrong with you, Flynn? Can't you just be normal cranky?"

A few hours later, I had delivered three of my passengers to their next destination at a lodge on the outskirts of Willow Brook, Alaska, and was planning to head straight back home with Daphne. When she asked to go along today because she wanted to see the mountain range again, I'd said yes, thinking we'd have company. I'd inconveniently forgotten our company was only for the first leg of the trip.

While I was making sure the compartment under the plane was properly secured, my cell phone rang. Since we were near Willow Brook, there was decent reception.

I quickly slipped the phone out of my pocket. "Flynn here," I said.

"Hey Flynn, it's Nate Fox. Heard you were at the airport in Willow Brook and about to head south."

"Yep. That's my flight plan, heading back to my place near Diamond Creek."

"I need a favor."

Although Alaska was geographically sprawling, there was a tight-knit sense of community amongst the residents in the small towns scattered across the state. The sense of community was even tighter in some professions, particularly that of bush pilots. We shared a sense of purpose and were often the link for many people to friends, family, supplies, medical treatment, and more.

Although we didn't see each other very often, I'd known Nate for years. If he needed a favor, I wouldn't hesitate. And I knew he'd do the same for me.

"Whatever it is, you got it."

Nate chuckled. "That's faith, dude."

"I trust you not to ask me something ridiculous."

"We have some food and supplies for Henry Stanson waiting for delivery. Do you mind dropping them off at his place on your way?"

Henry owned a remote fishing and hunting lodge between Willow Brook and Diamond Creek. Considering it was only a slight detour, it would be an easy favor.

Less than an hour later, I was maneuvering my

plane up into the air with the delivery of food and supplies. The wind was kicking up a bit, and the plane bounced slightly in the air. I glanced toward Daphne, but she seemed completely unruffled.

"You enjoying the view?" I called over the loud rumble of the engine.

Daphne glanced at me with a broad smile on her face. "I love it! Thanks for letting me tag along today."

My mouth was curling into a smile before I could stop it. "Anytime."

By the time we landed at the next lodge, the wind was bad. With it being late summer and bumping up against autumn in Alaska, it was getting cooler in the afternoons and evenings. When we climbed out of the plane, the wind was chilly enough that Daphne curled her arms around her waist and stomped her feet on the ground.

"Wow, it got cold fast," she said over the wind.

We were deep in the Kenai Mountains. As the crow flew, we were roughly an hour away from home and a few thousand feet higher. It was windy enough that I wasn't sure it was smart to take off again.

Without being asked, Daphne started to help me unload the boxes. Much as she gave off a princess vibe, she didn't like to be idle. If there was something to do, she was jumping in to do it.

Henry came jogging out of the lodge. "Need some help with those?"

"There are two boxes left in the plane," I replied, gesturing with my chin over my shoulder.

I'd delivered supplies here before, so I knew to go into Henry's lodge and hook a right into an industrial-sized storage area for food and goods. Not much later, we stood in the entryway of his lodge.

Henry was a longtime Alaskan. He'd moved here in

his twenties and was now pushing eighty. He operated a minimalist fishing lodge, much less luxurious than the resort I ran. Henry's place was nuts and bolts. He served exclusively those guests who wanted to hunt and fish. There were no viewing tours or any extras.

Due to how long he'd been here, he was also generally unfazed by Alaska's occasional extreme weather. I grew up here, so not much weather worried me. Being in the south-central part of the state meant we experienced less of the brutal and frigid cold than the northern part, but we got plenty of wind, rain, and snow. The wind could be a ruthless devil when you were in the air in a small plane.

Henry met my eyes. "If I were you, I'd stay put. I just checked the forecast. The wind's picking up, and the storm's going to last through the night. Rain and fog are already on the way."

I knew perfectly well that Henry's suggestion was the right thing to do. I simply didn't know how Daphne would feel about an overnight here. When I glanced her way, my eyes collided with hers just as she looked up at me.

A hint of anxiety swirled in the jade green depths of her gaze, but then she lifted her chin. Fuck me. It was getting worse. Whenever she lifted her chin like that, a stubborn little motion, it turned me on.

"Henry's right. You okay sitting tight for the night?" I asked.

"Of course," she said, her voice squeaking at the end.

———

Roughly a half an hour later, Daphne and I stared at each other across the bed.

"It'll be fine. I'll sleep on the floor," she offered.

"You're not sleeping on the fucking floor, princess," I replied, my words coming out harsher than I intended. I glanced down at the floor in question. It was hardwood and uninviting. Looking back at her, I shrugged. "I'm not either. We'll share the bed, and it'll be fine. I promise I don't bite. If necessary, you can put some pillows between us. For now, let's grab something to eat." I didn't even wait for her reply as I left the room.

Chapter Nine

DAPHNE

Flynn's words echoed in my mind. *You're not sleeping on the fucking floor, princess.*

Since the discovery that only one room was available for us to share at this rather utilitarian lodge, my mind had been frantically trying to come up with a way to deal with the situation. My brain was like a hamster on a wheel, spinning and spinning and spinning with nowhere to go.

Now, it was the middle of the night, and I'd awoken to that barrier of pillows completely obliterated. I couldn't even blame Flynn. I must've kicked them out of the way and was now latched on to him like he was my personal teddy bear.

He was warm and hard all over. After weeks of practically salivating and wondering just what his body looked like underneath his clothes, I was now currently plastered against it. Although I couldn't see it, I most assuredly could feel it.

His arm was wrapped around my back, his big palm curled over my bottom with his fingers almost brushing between my thighs. My hand rested over one of his pecs, and before I could even stop myself, my fingers went exploring. Because I couldn't help my curiosity.

Oh hell, who was I kidding? In this quiet darkness with the wind rushing at the house in gusts, I felt as if my heart was beating in tune with the storm outside. I wanted Flynn. Life and its messiness had convinced me I might never experience desire again, so the headiness of wanting him was intense.

I hadn't laid a hand on Flynn until now. Like light suddenly flooding a darkened room when a shade was opened, my desire rushed in where I'd thought I'd lost all capacity for it. My cheeks were so hot I knew my face would be bright pink if anyone could see me. The thaw had begun inside me the very day I'd met Flynn. For more than one night, I'd brought myself to climax with my fingers while imagining him.

Those same fingers traced over his chest and shoulders before mapping lower. Oh wow. He had a true six-pack. I could count the hard ridges with my fingers.

I nearly jumped out of my skin at the sound of his voice, like rough velvet in the night. "What are you doing, Daphne?"

Flynn didn't move or say anything else, but I could feel his body's shift to being awake. A subtle tension thrummed through him, and his heart thudded against his ribs. I had no doubt he could feel my heart beating wildly against his side.

"I don't know," I lied.

Even though the polite and proper voice in my mind was screaming at me, I didn't move. It felt as if an electric current was circulating between Flynn and me. Sparks skittered over the surface of my skin, and liquid need slid through my veins. The air was abruptly in short supply in the room. I could hardly get more than a shallow sip in my lungs.

I expected Flynn to notice his hand was cupping my bottom and shove me away. The man had been nothing but distant and cranky with me. At his best, I got something akin to a smile.

"So much for your pillow barrier," he murmured.

An almost hysterical laugh bubbled up in my throat. I tried to keep it from escaping, but a little bit slipped out. Flynn surprised me when I felt the rumble of a laugh in his chest under my palm—because, yeah, my hand was still on his chest. His chest was incredible—his skin warm and sleek with a dusting of hair. All hard planes that I wanted to explore with my hands and my tongue, if I was being completely honest.

"Wow, princess, you laughed."

For the first time ever, the nickname he called me didn't irritate me. I laughed again. I finally dared a glance at him, resting my chin on my hand over his chest.

Some kind of fluorescent night-light glowed in the corner of the room. He'd attempted to turn it off last night, but apparently, it was impossible to turn off. That little silvery stretch of light from the corner cast his face mostly in shadow, but I could see his eyes. They locked on mine the moment I looked toward him. I didn't know what to think of any of this.

I was aroused beyond belief. I could feel the slick heat of it at the apex of my thighs. I knew the moment I looked into Flynn's gaze that he was aroused too. His eyes searched mine. Although the room was quiet, the storm raged outside, coming at the roof in a rhythmic give and take. Rain struck sharply against the window beside the bed.

Blood rushed through my ears with every beat of my heart. I could feel Flynn's answering heartbeat thudding hard and fast. I could also feel the edge of his hard, hot cock barely brushing my knee where it rested over his hip. Because I had truly plastered myself to his side, practically climbing him in my sleep.

"Tell me what you want, princess."

Flynn's voice came out husky and thick, and his words shocked me. While I may not have understood why I wanted him so fiercely, I knew it down to my bones. Every cell in my body was attuned to him.

With the force of my desire humming through me, in the darkness of this room in a place I'd never been, with a storm cascading outside around us, my usual barriers fell away. I spoke the plain truth. "You."

I felt the leap of Flynn's heart against my palm when I spoke that single word. As his eyes searched mine in that thin, silvery light, I braced myself. What he said next surprised me. "Okay." He said it easily, his tone relaxed and nothing like the usually curt way he spoke to me. "That works because I want you too."

A little thrill raced through me at his blunt, direct statement. Surprising myself once again, I shimmied closer and dropped a kiss right at the little divot at the base of his throat. I wanted to taste him, so I did.

After that, I dropped another kiss on the side of his neck, and my tongue darted out this time. He smelled woodsy and crisp with the fresh scent of soap clinging to him from the shower I knew he'd taken earlier.

Need pierced me so sharply when he let out a rough growl that I could hardly bear it. His hand gave my bottom a squeeze and then swept up my back in a rough, heated pass. His fingers slid through my hair as he cupped the nape of my neck and drew me closer to him. I didn't mind one bit that he pulled me over his body, and my knees fell to the sides so I was straddling him.

I hadn't planned it that way, but I could feel the tease of his cock through his boxers, just barely grazing between my thighs. I let out an inelegant moan.

Flynn's low chuckle sent my belly into spinning flips, and I saw the flash of his smile in the darkness.

Just before his lips met mine, he spoke, "Don't get bossy, princess. I'm in charge."

When I opened my mouth to argue the point, my words were lost because he fit his mouth to mine. He tugged me closer and swept his tongue inside in one deep stroke.

I was *waaaay* out of practice with kissing, with anything even remotely related to flirting, romance, or sex. That said, I was instantly confident Flynn was the best kisser in the entire universe.

I melted into him with every stroke of his tongue against mine. He angled my head to the side and kissed me so masterfully I was pretty sure I was going to go up into flames. I wouldn't even care. I wanted to dive into this fire and burn to ash if only Flynn kept on kissing me.

His tongue stroked mine almost lazily. He was in no hurry at all. He alternated those deep, overpowering kisses with drawing back to drop hot kisses on the corners of my lips, to nip lightly on my bottom lip, and to murmur all kinds of indecipherable things. I couldn't even process the words, but I knew how they felt—naughty, flirty, dirty, and somehow sweet.

I barely registered as he shifted us until I was on my back, my hair in a tangle on the pillows, and one of his hands pushing my T-shirt up. The calloused surface of his palm on my skin sent sparks flying, rising in the air and then falling over me again as I tried to catch my breath and frantically absorb every sensation.

"Mmm, princess," he murmured against my belly, the stubble on his cheeks yet another sensation that made me feel hot and needy. I shifted my legs restlessly, my clit throbbing. I was so wet my arousal had saturated my silk panties.

"You're so fucking beautiful." He rose up on an elbow to cup one of my bare breasts. My nipple was already tight and achy, begging for his touch. He gave it to me, rolling it between his thumb and forefinger, then brushing back and forth over it in a teasing touch.

I gasped, and cried out, "Flynn!"

"Right here, princess." He teased my other breast as my hips rocked against his thigh where it rested between my knees. "Open your eyes."

I dragged my eyelids up to find him watching me. "I want to see those gorgeous eyes when you come," he murmured.

Oh. My. God. He was so blunt and direct, and it turned me on more than I ever could have imagined. His hand slipped over my trembling belly to cup my mound. I rocked restlessly.

"You want me," he teased. "You really do, princess. My, oh my."

"I already said that," I gasped when he teased a finger lightly over the wet silk, his touch grazing over my clit and making me bite my lip to keep from crying out.

In another second, he pushed the silk out of the way, and two fingers trailed through my folds. I was slippery wet and had absolutely no shame.

"Flynn, please," I begged between pants as he rubbed his fingers back and forth, just grazing over my swollen clit.

"Open your eyes," he demanded, repeating his husky command.

I was nearly out of my mind with need, but I obeyed and was instantly ensnared in his gaze. He sank one finger knuckle deep inside me and then added another, the feel of it pushing me to near delirium. My vision blurred as I struggled to stay focused on him.

"You feel so good, princess," he murmured, watching me intently as he moved his fingers in and out of my very core.

My hips rocked into every stroke as I chased my sweet release. Pressure built and built, tightening inside until I was trembling all over.

"Give it to me." His husky command pushed me over the edge.

My eyes finally closed as my head fell back into the pillows. A rush of pleasure cascaded through me and intensified when I felt his tongue swirling around my clit as he sucked on it lightly. My climax went on and on as shudders wracked me.

By the time it was over, I'd practically forgotten who I was and where I was. I'd forgotten everything but Flynn.

My awareness came in fragments, and I felt Flynn's light touch when his palm coasted over my belly. He pressed a kiss on the side of one breast before he pulled my T-shirt down.

Chapter Ten

FLYNN

Rain lashed against the windows. The wind rushed through this valley, rolling in rhythmic swells over the roof. My internal state was just as unsettled, if not more so.

It felt as if the storm itself had taken residence in my body. Lust lashed at me with as much force as the wind and rain outside. Daphne—uptight princess— was absolutely breathtaking when she let her guard down. She'd utterly slayed me.

During this dark, stormy night while we were cocooned in our own space, I forgot the weight of everything I carried inside. I'd also greatly underestimated the effect Daphne could have on me.

Her skin was silky and warm. The temptation to take things further was nearly impossible to resist. I called upon every ounce of discipline I had and shoved against it.

Rising on an elbow, I all but yanked Daphne's T-shirt down and folded her into my arms. I could feel her heartbeat where her rib cage pressed against my chest. As hers beat a rapid pace, mine echoed through my body, and I slowly caught my breath.

Jesus fucking Christ. We hadn't even taken things further. I hadn't even buried myself inside her, but I knew the very core of her was welcoming, slick, and clenching. I was out of breath, stunned, and rattled beyond measure. My control was absolute. Except, apparently, when it came to Daphne.

When Henry commented it was lucky we could share a room, mistakenly thinking Daphne and I were a couple, I'd almost wanted to argue the point. When he further mentioned it was the only room available, I didn't want to make a scene. I wasn't about to freeze my ass off and sleep on a wooden floor, nor allow Daphne to do so. I figured I would have no problem with the barrier of pillows she put between us at the start of the night. It was just sleeping, after all.

Yet sleep suddenly felt deeply intimate. If I shoved Daphne away now, I knew there would only be questions, so I played it cool.

"Flynn?" Daphne's voice was soft and frayed on the edges.

I silently reminded myself to stay calm.

"Yeah?"

"I feel selfish."

"About what?"

I felt her eyes on me in the darkness and opened mine. The moment I met her gaze in the shadowy room, my heart felt a physical pull toward her, and there was a tug low in my gut. An overwhelming rush of uncertainty washed over me.

I steeled myself, and repeated, "About what?"

The light was too dim for me to know for certain, but I was pretty sure she blushed. And I knew just how fucking cute she was when she blushed. "Yes, princess?" I prompted.

She sighed and elbowed me lightly in the side of my ribs. "When I said I wanted you, I didn't mean for it to be a one-way street," she finally said.

Damn. *This* woman. Although she was guarded and uptight, she was so damn honest that it chipped away at the ice around my heart.

"I know, but I don't think we should take things further."

I could feel her eyes searching mine. I didn't quite understand how she could see so deep inside me. It felt as if she climbed right into my heart.

No matter what she understood, she didn't comment on it. "Oh, okay."

She held my gaze for a long moment, something flickering in her eyes before she nodded and let her head fall back against the pillows.

I fell asleep with Daphne curled up beside me. Although I tried to tell my brain this was a bad idea, I couldn't bring myself to let her go.

She felt so exquisitely good. And I was so incredibly tired of holding everyone at bay.

Four days later

"You have got to be fucking kidding me."

Cat gave me a saucy shrug paired with a roll of her eyes. "Nope, not kidding."

"Fuck!"

My other sister, Nora, came striding in the kitchen

at the resort and cast me a pointed look. "I thought we were trying not to swear so much."

Cat burst out laughing. "It's a lost cause with Flynn. I think we should have a swear jar so I can at least make some money out of this."

"Please, go get ready for school," I muttered, resting my elbows on the counter and tunneling my hands through my hair.

Blessedly, Cat left the room. Lifting my head, I met Nora's gaze.

"What happened?" she asked.

"That woman I hired to cook, quit. Just fucking left."

"You mean Tonya?"

"Yeah, Tonya. She up and left this morning without even cooking breakfast."

I eyed the clock above the door. It was going on six thirty a.m. Pretty soon, we would have guests coming downstairs and expecting food.

Nora crossed her arms and gave me another pointed look. "Sometimes, you're an asshole to work for."

"I just need a cook. Is it that hard?"

I spun away from my sister just as Daphne entered the kitchen. She looked from me to Nora and back again. Meanwhile, I was busy trying to lock down the crazy that happened to my body any time she was near. The moment Daphne stepped into the room, every hair on my body stood on end. It felt as if electricity zipped back and forth in the air between us.

"I can cook," Daphne said.

In the four days that had elapsed since our night at Henry's lodge and the interlude that had literally been burned into my brain, Daphne and I had settled into a silent agreement to pretend it never happened. Small problem, though. There was no ignoring the chemistry that just wouldn't quit.

I had plenty to do to keep me occupied and plenty of other guests at the resort to deal with. Of course, I also had my nosy, opinionated, and way too perceptive for my own sanity siblings to handle.

Speaking of. Nora caught my eye with a knowing glint in hers, but I ignored it. Maybe it was crazy to take Daphne up on her offer, but I didn't have time to figure this out. In the next twenty minutes, I needed to be out the door for a flightseeing trip. Those trips made us money, the money I needed to throw into Cat's college fund and everything else. Fucking money.

"Can you really cook, princess?"

"Does he call you princess all the time?" Nora interjected.

Daphne was unfazed and shrugged when she looked at Nora. "Not all the time, but sometimes." Her eyes met mine again. "Yes, I can really cook. It might shock you to learn that some people say I'm excellent at it. I used to run a bakery."

I had questions—lots of them—because, despite my best efforts, I was relentlessly curious about Daphne. Even before that night, it hadn't slipped my notice that she'd make a damn good poker player. She held her cards close to her chest all the time. I sensed there was more than a typical story behind her choice to come to Alaska on her own. If I lost the battle to my curiosity, I'd find out all her secrets. Not now, though.

"All right then. If you can cover the meals for today, I would seriously owe you one."

"What he means is he'll pay you," Nora chimed in helpfully.

"I'll take care of it. Are you—?" I began.

Daphne was already striding into the massive pantry and waved dismissively over her shoulder. "Flynn, I have this. I can whip something up in no time. I don't need instructions or any help. I promise."

My sister snorted a laugh, and I cast a glare in her direction.

Following Daphne to the pantry, I leaned my shoulder against the inside of the doorframe. "Thank you."

She already had a bag of flour hooked in an elbow and was rummaging through the industrial-sized refrigerator. Straightening, she closed the refrigerator door and looked in my direction. "You're welcome. I promise, the kitchen is where I'm most competent."

I wanted to say something. In the weeks she'd been here, it was obvious Daphne was up close and personal with self-doubt. At this moment, she seemed calm, collected, and confident. I wanted to point that out, but that would be weird, so I simply said, "Thank you. Really."

Daphne nodded just as my brother, Grant, called from the other room. "Where the hell is Flynn?"

"You better get going."

I left. Although I'd been surprised at her announcement that she could cook, I didn't doubt Daphne was excellent at it. She wouldn't have said as much if she weren't. I didn't know many things about her, but Daphne either said nothing or told the truth.

Chapter Eleven

DAPHNE

After three days of cooking and baking for the resort guests, I felt better than I had in years. Mind you, the bar was so low on my well-being that it wasn't hard to beat, but still. It felt good to feel useful, and it felt good to remember there were some things I could manage.

It said something that I felt that good despite how unnerved I was by the insanity of what had passed between Flynn and me during that stormy night. It was hard not to think about it. It was nearly impossible to forget when he was always around and always mouthwateringly handsome.

Take now, for example. Flynn was standing at the counter, picking up a piece of cheese Grant had sliced into giant chunks. When my eyes snagged on Flynn's long fingers, I instantly recalled the feel of them. Inside me. My eyes—willful, disobedient, and greedy—traced the flex of his forearm as he lifted the cheese to his mouth.

Yeah, forearms. I thought Flynn's forearms were

totally hot. That was how bad I had it. I purposely took a moment to study Grant's forearms from where he stood beside Flynn. He drained a glass of water and set it down. The flex of his forearms did nothing for me. It was actually kind of boring to stare at his forearms.

"I think Daphne should do it," Cat said as she skipped into the kitchen and slid across the floor in her socks to stop at Flynn's side.

Flynn tweaked her ponytail with his free hand. "Daphne should do what?"

"Stay on as the full-time chef," Cat said blithely as if that made perfect sense.

Nora, whom apparently Cat had been talking with before she came into the kitchen, followed her in. "I'm not having much luck with applicants. You're kind of an asshole sometimes," she said, resting a hand on her hip and narrowing her eyes at Flynn. "Diamond Creek isn't that big, and word travels. Marley at the ski lodge told me that Harry heard from the last woman you hired that you told her she was too slow."

I bit my lip to keep from laughing when Nora's eyes met mine as she winked. Grant snorted a laugh but offered no more.

"We all know you probably did, so don't even bother arguing," Nora added.

Flynn sighed. "I hope Harry didn't hire her. They do a much faster business at the restaurant than we do. Tonya didn't know how to hurry to save her life."

"I'll do it." Those words just flew out of my mouth without my permission.

Flynn spun around, giving me an intent, searching look. "Aren't you due to fly out at the end of this week?"

"It doesn't matter. I don't have to go back."

I was suddenly flustered under Flynn's gaze, which felt like an X-ray into my soul. Maybe I hadn't planned on blurting that out, and maybe it was crazy. But maybe it was also exactly what I needed.

"Okay, princess, you're hired," he said flatly.

Daphne stared at me, pink tingeing her cheeks before she looked down at the pan in front of her and turned off the burner flame underneath it. When her auburn lashes swept up again, she lifted her chin slightly, and a jolt of electricity sizzled down my spine. I'd just lost my mind.

Cat squealed, abruptly reminding me I wasn't alone with Daphne. She had the strangest effect on me, causing me to instantly forget other people were nearby. I hadn't laid a finger on her—hell, I hadn't even gotten within a foot of her—since my temporary break from reality that night. It didn't matter; nothing seemed to cool my ardor for her.

I stuffed another piece of cheese in my mouth and walked out of the kitchen with Grant trailing me.

"Good choice. Daphne's the best cook we've ever had, and you don't even yell at her." I looked his way only to collide with the sly glint in his eyes and a teasing grin. "All you gotta do is keep your hands off her."

Chapter Thirteen

DAPHNE

"Oh, come on," Nora implored. "I need the company. Plus, you haven't even been to the lodge restaurant. You need to investigate the competition."

"Competition?" I looked out the windows where I saw nothing but mountains, trees, and the ocean in the distance. "I don't really think a restaurant at a ski lodge twenty miles away is competition."

Nora glared at me. "What do I have to do to guilt you into going with me? I don't want to go on my own because I have a ton of errands to do, and errands are boring."

"All you had to do was say that. I don't need to be guilted. What time?"

"Will this afternoon work?"

At my nod, Nora's brown eyes twinkled with her smile. "Awesome. I'll come find you." She paused, her gaze flicking down to my shirt. "You might want to change that."

I looked down at said shirt. Flour was dusted across the front because I'd started kneading dough without remembering to put on my apron. That wasn't the problem, though. There was a giant splash of coffee as an accent over one of my breasts.

I glared at it. "I didn't even notice. Thanks for the heads-up."

I hurried off and wasn't paying attention as I began jogging up the spiral staircase. Apparently, Flynn wasn't looking either as he began to descend. We'd done an admirable job of avoiding each other for the past few weeks. Ever since "that night" as I'd come to think of it, I'd studiously tried to keep my distance. I'd also tried not to think too much about it.

While I had succeeded in keeping my distance, I'd utterly and completely failed at not thinking about it. Flynn filled my thoughts, crowding out everything else when I had a spare minute.

And here we were, about to collide on the spiral staircase. My only options were to back down and look like a coward or shimmy sideways to get past him.

"Excuse me." Dear God, my voice came out raspy

As I turned sideways to go by, my foot caught on a tread, and I stumbled. Flynn, being the steady, strong man he was, caught me with one hand on my hip and the other on my shoulder when I stumbled into him.

"Easy there," he murmured.

Now, I was literally plastered against him, and my nipples stood at attention. There was nowhere for me to jump back, and I knew my cheeks were bright red when I looked up at him.

"Sorry," I said breathlessly.

My feet seemed genuinely stuck in place. My only solace was that Flynn didn't seem to be moving either. Considering he'd been avoiding me just as thoroughly as I'd been avoiding him, I didn't think he was doing that on purpose.

For a flicker, I thought he was going to kiss me. My body was practically leaning into it as my eyes tore free from his tractor beam of a gaze and landed on his lips.

Oh, sweet hell. I knew exactly how good of a kisser Flynn was. I also knew he could work magic with his mouth just about anywhere on my body. I had a vivid and piercing memory of the feel of his mouth closing over one of my aching nipples as his fingers teased into my slick core in the darkness of that rainy night. Heat rushed through me, and my heart started pounding so hard and so fast, I was certain he could hear it.

"Flynn!" someone called.

My breath came out in a startled huff. I instinctively tried to jump back, only to lose my balance again on the stairs. Flynn, being the rescue-y kind of guy he was, steadied me again.

The two points where his hands were on me—my left hip and my right shoulder—felt branded, the heat of his touch so intense it sent sparks scattering through my entire body.

"Flynn!" the voice called again.

"I think someone needs you," I whispered.

"Yeah. That's Grant."

He eased his hands off me. We didn't speak again as I finally shimmied past him with my heart rioting in my chest, and my panties wet.

Hurrying into my room, I caught myself before I actually slammed the door shut. I wasn't slamming it out of anger. The momentum of my frazzled nerves and the driving beat of my pulse had my body so revved up, everything was happening too fast and too hard.

I stopped in the center of my room and closed my eyes, willing my out of control pulse and the heat racing through my body to slow down. I was practicing deep breathing techniques I'd learned in therapy just to get a hold of myself after a close encounter with Flynn. That was how bad I had it.

I'd dived off the deep end when it came to him. That night, which I hadn't been able to resist, had been a bout of pure insanity. I kept telling myself it never would've happened if I hadn't been so out of my element.

Opening my eyes, I squeezed my hands into tight little fists and released them before swinging my arms like windmills. That was another trick I'd learned when I was deep in grief, under a crushing weight I didn't think I could ever shake off my chest. My therapist had told me to use my body as a tool of distraction to nudge my thoughts out of the ruts in my brain. It actually worked, even when I didn't believe it could.

After a few jumping jacks, I hurried across my room to the small closet and pulled out a clean shirt. I didn't worry all that much about how I looked when I was working, but I tried not to sport too many spills. As I tugged it over my head, I realized I was impatient for the day to pass. I was looking forward to dinner with Nora. In all honesty, I was quite curious about the social life of Diamond Creek.

Although I'd driven into town a few times on my own and once or twice to do errands with Cat, who was always a good volunteer and ever helpful at carrying things and keeping track of what we needed for the kitchen, I hadn't spent much time there just for fun. When I hurried down the spiral staircase, Flynn wasn't blocking my way this time, so I made it downstairs with no trouble.

One thing Alaska was teaching me was that I could survive on my own. Although my choice to come here was serendipitous, and frankly random, it was turning out to be good for me. With the exception of my confused and endless desire for Flynn.

FLYNN

Angling my plane in the air, I looked ahead at the glacier tucked between two mountain peaks, glowing and otherworldly blue under the sunshine. I heard a few oohs and aahs from the back of the plane and angled to the side to offer a better view. I was flying along the mountains encircling Kachemak Bay before returning to Diamond Creek.

Most of this area was undeveloped, especially on the far side of the bay. There were a few Alaska Native villages scattered on the shores, along with Seldovia, which was one of the oldest towns in the area.

I'd flown this group to Seldovia for the morning to tour the picturesque little town. Inside of a half hour, I had landed and taxied the plane into the hangar after everyone disembarked. It was late afternoon, and I went through my usual routine of checking everything on the plane before leaving for the day. I was putting a few things away in our storage room there when I heard someone call my name.

Leaning my head out, I saw Elias approaching. "In here," I called.

His head swiveled in my direction, the sound of his footsteps echoing in the cavernous space as he crossed to me. Stopping inside the doorway and resting his shoulder on the frame, he asked, "How many trips do we have tomorrow?"

"Four. I have you slated to take two. That gonna work?"

Elias nodded. "Yeah. Just sorting my schedule mentally. My mom's flying in tomorrow evening."

"Oh, that's right. She's staying out at the resort, right?"

"Of course. Be prepared for her to be as nosy as usual," he offered with a chuckle.

"She flying in to Diamond Creek or Anchorage?"

"All the way to Diamond Creek. I arranged her flights."

"She'll be glad to see you." I zipped up my day bag and slung it over my shoulder. "You drive or ride with Gabriel?"

"I hitched a ride with him this morning. I was hoping I could hitch a ride back with you."

"You know you don't even need to ask," I replied as we turned and walked out together. "You mind if I stop and get some coffee?"

"Of course not."

A few minutes later, we were in line at Red Truck Coffee. Cammi was noticeably absent today, and the guy she had covering for her looked a bit overwhelmed. When we got to the front of the line, Elias was short with him.

Catching the guy's eyes, I quipped, "Don't take it personally. He's just out of sorts because Cammi isn't here."

I heard Elias almost choke on his coffee and

turned to whack him on the back helpfully. "I'm sure she'll be back tomorrow, right?"

The guy nodded. "Yeah, she's moving, so she's got me here while she rounds up people to help her with that. She'll be back bright and early tomorrow. I hope the coffee is okay."

I took a swallow. "Delicious, as always." I slid the kid an extra tip.

Elias remained silent throughout this exchange. When we got back in my truck, he said, "Fuck you."

I arched a brow and started my truck. "You don't wanna fuck me; you wanna fuck Cammi."

"Yeah, just like you wanna fuck Daphne."

Elias never pulled any punches, and this was not the first time he'd given me shit about Daphne.

Little did he know I'd been insane enough to act on my totally inappropriate and ridiculous attraction to Daphne. A jolt sizzled through me at the mere mention of Daphne, and I instantly recalled her body shuddering in my arms. I didn't know what I'd been thinking that night. I suppose I hadn't been thinking. At all. Even worse, I was coming to regret that I hadn't taken things all the way. Some stupid and misplaced sense of honor stopped me and held me in check.

Now, I didn't know if I'd ever get that chance again. I *did* know the chemistry wouldn't fucking quit between us. I focused on the road as I turned. "So what if I do? You're not Cammi's boss. You can have your way with her. Plus, I think she likes you too."

Elias narrowed his eyes at me when I glanced his way. "For fuck's sake, don't you dare turn into a matchmaker."

I chuckled. "I could say the same to you."

I felt his shrug. "Whatever. Plus, I don't think it's

that big of a deal that you're Daphne's boss. It's not like there's an HR department to chase you down."

As I slowed to turn onto the road that would lead us to the highway, the sound of a honking horn drew my attention. Looking to my left, I saw my sister Nora waving madly in her truck with Daphne in the passenger seat.

I stared a beat too long, and Elias interjected, "See? One look at her and you're stunned."

Turning, I cuffed him lightly on the shoulder. "Fuck you."

"You don't wanna fuck me; you wanna fuck Daphne." He laughed as he threw my own words back at me. With him laughing too hard, I lifted a hand to wave at Nora and Daphne, biting my cheeks to keep from wondering aloud where they were going.

Chapter Fifteen

DAPHNE

"Oh, my God," I moaned, speaking just as I finished swallowing. "This food is divine. If I was trying to run a restaurant here in Diamond Creek, this would be serious competition. Actually, it would be serious competition anywhere."

I took another bite of the balsamic glazed salmon, savoring every second it was in my mouth. "How's yours?" I asked as I paused to take a sip of wine.

"Divine, just like you said." Nora had gotten the halibut tacos. I'd already taken a few bites and offered her some of my salmon in return. Halibut tacos were a distinctly Alaskan dish and scrumptious. The creamy and subtle fish was perfect with cilantro and peach salsa.

Nora took another bite and leaned back in her chair. "I need to slow down. I can't overdo it and ruin the amazing. I have to say, though, your food is just as good as this."

"You don't need to shower me with compliments," I said before taking another bite of my salmon.

"I know I don't need to, but I just want you to

know your food is freaking amazing. If I understand right, you once ran a bakery. Is that so?"

"True story. It was my big accomplishment. I love to cook. It worked out perfectly that your last cook quit. I get to do what I love without the pressure of running an actual restaurant."

Nora took another bite of her halibut tacos and then eyed me speculatively. "Can I be nosy?" she asked with a grin teasing the corners of her mouth.

"I'm pretty sure you're just going to be nosy anyway, but I'll give you permission since you asked," I returned dryly.

Nora laughed just as a woman approached our table. It wasn't the man who seated us or the young woman who waited on us. Nora clearly knew her, though, because her face broke into a wide smile. "Hey, Delia." She stood and pulled the woman into a quick hug. "This is my friend Daphne," she said, gesturing to me. I didn't know if I counted as Nora's friend, but my heart warmed a little at having her describe me as one. "She's our new chef."

I started to stand, and Delia waved me back in my chair. "No need to get up. I've heard your food is amazing," she said, her blue eyes twinkling. With her honey-blond hair and warm smile, Delia was simply lovely.

"You've heard about my food?" Anxiety spun in my chest. Although the kitchen was one area where I felt confident, it was always intimidating to wonder what other skilled chefs might think. Having come from a city where trying to start a new restaurant was a cutthroat business, I'd been enjoying my anonymity here.

Delia's eyes twinkled. "Of course. I'm sure you feel like you're in the middle of nowhere out there, but you're only twenty minutes away. All of the guests come to Diamond Creek for shopping and more food."

"We love her, and I told Flynn not to be an asshole to her," Nora piped up.

My laughter bubbled out. "He's stayed out of my way so far."

"He knows a good chef when he's found one," Nora said firmly. "By the way, did you hire the last chef we had who quit?" Her eyes swung to Delia.

Delia shook her head. "Marley told me that she actually complained about Flynn at the interview. Although I'm not here to defend Flynn, that's never a good look."

Nora nodded while I remained silent, thinking there wasn't much for me to offer on that point. Delia glanced back at me. "Welcome to the area. If you keep turning out food as good as the rumors say, I don't think you'll need to worry about Flynn being a jerk to you."

Delia departed with a light squeeze on my shoulder, immediately stopping to check on another table as she moved away.

"She seems really nice," I offered after taking a sip of my wine.

"Delia's great. Although we both grew up around here, I didn't really get to know her until the past few years. She was a few years ahead of me in school, and you know how that goes. Anyway, she manages the restaurant here. She was a single mom for years, but then she fell in love with Garrett Hamilton, whose family owns this ski lodge. He's a hotshot attorney who moved up here from Seattle. His brother, Gage, runs this place with his wife. Garrett came up for a vacation and fell in love with Delia. It was all very romantic," Nora explained. "It's nice to see her doing so well. And if she's heard about your food, that's a good sign."

I rolled my eyes. "I appreciate the compliments as much as anyone, but it's not a business issue. The people are going to eat there no matter what. They might come to Diamond Creek for lunch or dinner occasionally but..." My words trailed off with a shrug.

"I know, but we like the food to be good. You do seem to be immune to Flynn's attitude," she offered with a cheeky smile.

"I don't know about that. He gets cranky; he just doesn't snap at me too much."

Nora looked as if she was considering something, but she simply lifted her water and took a swallow. "Do you like that wine?" she asked, gesturing to my wine glass. She was sticking with water since she was driving, but she'd insisted I try this particular wine.

"It's delicious. Did you say it's local?"

"Yes. It's from Diamond Creek Brewery. They make wine too. I keep telling Flynn we should buy from them occasionally, but he says it's too expensive. He worries about money constantly."

"I noticed."

I was so curious, *so* freaking curious about Flynn, but I wasn't about to get nosy with his sister about him.

Nora offered up answers anyway. "He worries because he came home to a bunch of debt. Grant had just started college, and I was in high school when our mom died. He put me and Grant through college, and he's raised Cat since she was nine. He's making sure he has enough saved up for her to go to college too. So I tease him, but he's the best big brother I could imagine. Even if he's cranky sometimes."

My heart did a funny tumble in my chest. I didn't need to go and think Flynn was amazing, in addition to being so sexy that I could hardly stop thinking about that one night between us.

"Wow," I said. "You're lucky to have him."

Nora nodded vigorously. "Yeah, he left the Air Force to come home. I think he was probably ready anyway. We all give him hell sometimes, but we're really protective of him."

Just when I thought Nora had forgotten to be nosy about me, she asked, "So what kind of life did you have that you could afford to come to Alaska for a month on your own? How could you change your plans to stay and work for us?"

"Well, that's more than a question," I said with a startled laugh.

Nora shrugged unabashedly. "I guess so. We all love you, and we're beyond happy you stayed."

"I'm pretty sure Flynn doesn't love me," I murmured.

Nora laughed at that. "He loves your food, he loves that you helped him out in a pinch, and he'll love you even more if you stay."

I took a gulp of my wine, twirling the glass in my fingers before I set it down. "My answer isn't simple. One thing I've learned in the past year is it's always better to be honest. It's kind of heavy, so if you don't want to hear it, that's okay."

Nora's gaze sobered as she looked back at me. "Tell me."

"To answer your first question, I was able to afford a month in Alaska after I closed my restaurant because I grew up with money." I lifted a shoulder in a shrug. "That's just luck. I don't think I deserve the money, or my family, for that matter. Trust me, I would trade the money if I could. My whole life kind of blew up about a year and a half ago. I had a son, Brandon. I was married, and I had my restaurant and friends. I thought my life was pretty good. Then Brandon was diagnosed with a rare form of brain cancer when he was four."

Nora's eyes widened, and she pressed her hand on her chest over her heart. "Oh, no. I'm so sorry."

I'd practiced saying this so many times that I could actually get through it without completely breaking down. My chest tended to feel a little hollow, but I could breathe, and my heart stubbornly kept on beating.

"Thank you. The survival rate for that cancer is not good at all. We knew almost right away that it wasn't likely he would live."

"What kind of cancer?" Nora asked softly.

"Medulloepithelioma. It's rare and usually diagnosed in young children. Five months is the average survival rate."

I swallowed through the painful knot in my throat as the tears wicked from it. Blinking rapidly, I pushed ahead. "He died four months later."

Nora reached across the table and caught my hand in hers. We weren't close, at least not yet, but her touch was so warm and so heartfelt, and that alone almost had me crying.

I kept it together and forged on. "All of that was awful, and I wouldn't wish it on anyone. But the month before Brandon died, I found out my husband was having an affair with one of my closest friends."

"Oh, my God. That's just... it's just awful!" Nora looked horrified.

My anger usually buoyed me through this part of the explanation, and it did yet again. "Yeah, it was awful. He said it was because I was so emotionally unavailable. I don't know. I don't think I'll ever really know. I don't really think he loved me. In all honesty, I don't know that I really loved him. Maybe I loved the idea of what we had, but it was all exposed for the superficial sham that it was when something real happened. That last month was brutal. My friend, or rather my not-friend," I said with air quotes, "tried to apologize. She was horrified when it all came out because I didn't bother keeping it a secret. I was too raw. Keeping up appearances for somebody else's sake just didn't matter."

Nora was shaking her head, her eyes wide. "My God. Did she think you'd keep it a secret for her sake?"

"I don't really know. It doesn't matter to me either. After Brandon died, I kind of fell apart. I'd already closed my restaurant after we found out about Brandon's diagnosis, but I refused to go back to work for my family's business. My father runs an investment consortium, and my ex-husband's family is partners with him. My friend, who had an affair with my ex, worked there too. My father was nice enough to fire her, but he told me I had to deal with my ex, that he was too important for the company. I don't hate my parents, but I don't share their priorities. It's all business."

When I glanced over to gauge Nora's response, she was quiet, so I continued. "I saw a therapist for a while. When I finally had my shit together enough to be able to deal with anything, I wanted a change so extreme that maybe I could figure out what I wanted with life going forward. I found your resort almost by accident. There was an ad when I was searching online. I clicked on it and decided it was far enough away and so totally different from anything I'd ever done that maybe it was what I needed."

"I can't believe what you've been through," Nora breathed.

"I'm okay," I said. I meant it too. "As awful as all of it was, at least I didn't have to worry about paying the bills. I inherited some money from my grandmother, so that floated me. I can sleep through the night now. I still don't really know what I want to do long term, so you don't need to worry about me leaving my job anytime soon. Plus, I like it. Y'all don't have any expectations, so I'm just switching it up every day and doing whatever I want. It's fun."

Nora was looking really worried, with her brow knitted in concern and her eyes scanning my face. "Really, Nora, I'm okay. Either I lie to people about what happened, or I just tell the truth. I promised myself I was going to tell people the truth if they asked. You don't need to feel sorry for me. Period," I said firmly.

"Your son died. I just can't wrap my head around how hard that must've been."

"Oh, it was hard, all right. But I'm still here, and I can find joy. Loss is hard, no matter what. Your mother died when you were still in high school, right?"

"Well, yeah. That was hard, really hard. But she was my mom, not my child. Even though she died sooner than I ever wanted, you always expect your parents to go first."

"I don't think you can really compare situations. It's all relative. Instead of feeling sorry for me, tell me about your family."

Nora was quiet for a few beats before she dipped her chin in acknowledgment. "You're one of the strongest people I know. Okay, my family. Well, you know all of us. Flynn's the oldest by seven years. He has a different father, who we never knew. Our mom didn't have the greatest judgment in men, but she was amazing. Flynn's dad took off before he was even born. She raised him on her own until she met our dad. Then it was Grant, me, and Cat came last, but definitely not least."

I snorted a laugh. "Definitely not."

"Anyway, our dad was kind of an ass. He wasn't horrible, but he screwed around all the time and came and went pretty much as he pleased. Money-wise, we scraped by. My mom inherited this property from her parents after they passed. He was a builder, so they started on the resort and started the business, but then he left again. He actually died from a heart attack one day, leaving our mom with a ton of debt and a bunch of other problems. Flynn would send money whenever he could, but it's not like he made a ton in the military. Our mom had a genetic auto-immune disorder, and she eventually died from complications of that. I still miss her."

"I bet. I'm glad y'all have each other."

Nora smiled softly. "That we do. Sometimes we drive each other crazy, but Flynn held us all together. If he hadn't come home when our mother died, Cat and I might've ended up in foster care. Grant was in college, but he didn't have much money, and the court was concerned he couldn't financially support us. Flynn immediately intervened from a distance. They let us stay at the house since Grant came home from college. Flynn had to come home really fast. Then he had to deal with me when I was sixteen."

I smiled. "I bet that was fun."

Nora shrugged lightly. "It was. It's funny now, but I was probably a bitch."

"He loves you, that much is obvious." Because it was. Flynn might've been cranky with me, but his love for his family came through loud and clear in every action.

"My new goal is to find him a girlfriend," Nora commented.

I almost choked on the sip of wine I'd just taken. "Are you serious?"

"Yes! He needs to lighten up. Maybe if he gets laid, he will. It's all work, work, more work, and no play for him."

I decided to remain silent. I didn't even know what to think about the flash of possessiveness I experienced. I had *no* right to feel possessive about Flynn in any way.

It's just I wanted him all to myself. Even though I didn't believe I'd want anyone ever again. Not to mention, I was pretty sure he didn't consider me his type.

"Maybe you," Nora said as she eyed me with an assessing gaze.

"Oh, no," I said, holding a hand up. "Don't you dare try to set me up with anyone, much less Flynn."

"Well, the reason I think he doesn't get cranky with you in the kitchen is because he's totally got the hots for you."

My cheeks flamed, but I managed not to choke on my drink.

Chapter Sixteen

FLYNN

Late the following night, I drove through the darkness, watching as the moon rose above the mountains across the water. I'd taken an unplanned trip to Anchorage to pick up some plane engine parts after one of ours had some problems.

I figured that by the time I got back to the resort, everybody would be asleep. Although I hadn't necessarily wanted to take the extra trip, I'd been relieved for the change of pace. Last night, Nora had told me Daphne's story. I thought I was a hardened man. Seven years in the Air Force and two tours of active duty had taken me on some difficult journeys, yet nothing I'd faced felt as personally brutal as what Daphne went through.

This morning, I'd looked at her across the kitchen as she efficiently made breakfast for all of our guests and seamlessly multitasked while she prepped the upcoming meals for lunch and dinner. She'd lost her son and experienced a painful betrayal, and she was carrying on with that stubborn spark of cheer of hers. Like sunshine slipping through the cracks.

Somehow, knowing her history made me savor the nickname I'd given her. She did have that princess vibe. She'd gotten enough sass and spirit back to let it show.

When she turned and her stunning green eyes collided with mine across the room, my memory clicked onto that night of pure insanity. I didn't need to start *feeling* things about Daphne. So I hurried off, claiming I needed to check on two of our planes. I could always check on our planes, but the timing turned out right because one of them did have a problem.

We needed the rest of the planes for tourist trips, so I'd taken my trusty truck through the mountain pass to Anchorage. It was past midnight now as I turned off the highway onto the road that would lead me home. When I parked, I was surprised to see the lights on in the kitchen, but I figured someone had just left them on. The rest of the resort was quiet, and the motion sensor lights came on when my truck set them off.

My boots crunched in the gravel as I pocketed my keys. I ascended the steps quietly. After making my way through the back hallway into the entrance to my family's private quarters, I dropped my keys in the bowl on the table by the door. Nora had moved into a small house nearby last year, and Grant bounced between here and whoever's bed he happened to be warming. It was just Cat and me now. Cat's light was still on, so I reached in and flicked it off, looking over to see she'd fallen asleep while reading. I crossed the room and lifted the book off her chest, sliding her bookmark in and then leaving it on her bedside table.

I aimed for the kitchen to turn off the lights. When I opened the door, I was surprised to see

Daphne hard at work. In the weeks that had passed since I hired her impulsively, I'd discovered she was a relentlessly hard worker. She was usually up well before anyone else, making an array of baked goods for breakfast and usually worked until past dinner.

I took a moment to absorb her presence. Her hair was twisted into a messy knot on top of her head with tendrils hanging down around her neck. She wore an apron over a T-shirt and a pair of leggings. My eyes lingered on the curve of her hips and the dip at her waist.

My mouth watered at the thought of crossing the kitchen and dipping my head to drag my tongue along the side of her neck. Because I knew she tasted sweet. I also knew she smelled like sugar.

In an effort to distract myself, I called over, "Do you usually bake at night after the rest of us go to bed?"

Daphne jumped slightly and spun around, her hand flying to her chest. "Oh my God, you scared me!"

My common sense immediately forfeited in the battle with my need to be closer to her. I crossed the room, stopping only a few feet away from her.

"Sorry," I said, meaning it. "I didn't mean to scare you. But do you really work this late usually? Because I don't think I'm paying you enough as it is."

A wash of pink crested on her cheeks. She wrinkled her nose before shrugging lightly. "Sometimes. You don't need to pay me more. I like to bake."

"Do you like to sleep? Because you're up every day by five or so as far as I can tell."

I was teasing, but then I saw a flicker of something in Daphne's eyes. Before I could say anything else, she replied, "I'm not the best sleeper. When I can't sleep, I come down here and bake."

I wasn't thinking, or perhaps it was more that I'd thought too much about what Nora told me. Knowing she didn't sleep well, all I could think was that life had been far too brutally unfair to Daphne. My words got ahead of my brain. "I'm sorry about your son."

I knew something about sleepless nights just because of life. I could only imagine sleep was an elusive devil in the aftermath of what she'd gone through.

Daphne's eyes widened, and her breath came out in a startled puff. Watching her, I could almost see her metaphoric cloak of steel armor come down.

"Nora talked to you," she said, each word careful and measured.

"She did. I shouldn't have said anything." I didn't know how to step back from this and felt I'd walked into an intensely private moment without meaning to.

Daphne shook her head just barely, and her chin lifted incrementally. "I didn't ask her to keep it private. It's not a secret. It's just my messy life."

We stared at each other, and I contemplated the full picture of what Nora had shared with me—that after Daphne's son was diagnosed with an apparently god-awful type of cancer, she learned her husband was having an affair with her friend. What a fucking asshole. I wanted to personally slay her dragons.

Since she had, in a way, given me permission, I took a step closer. Because somehow, I needed her to know this. "Life sucks sometimes, and I'm so sorry. Your ex was stupid and an asshole. He didn't deserve you. You know that, right?"

Daphne's gorgeous eyes widened, her cheeks flushing a deep pink again. Her nostrils flared as she took a breath. "It doesn't really matter. It's the past."

It felt as if Daphne was trying to convince herself

as much as me. I couldn't say why, but I couldn't bear that someone had treated her so carelessly and cruelly.

Closing the distance between us in one long stride, I lifted a hand and caught a wayward lock of hair falling along her cheek. I brushed it back to tuck behind her ear.

"There's a reason I call you princess," I murmured.

Daphne's tongue darted out, swiping across her bottom lip before she asked, "There is?"

Just like that night, weeks ago now, it felt as if this moment was out of place and time. A moment set aside to forget all the reasons I shouldn't want Daphne with a need that rattled me to my bones.

"Because you are, to me, and you should be treated like one."

Daphne stared back at me. As I brushed my knuckles along the downy skin of her neck, I felt the wild flutter of her pulse.

"Oh," she said.

Because it seemed the only course of action in this particular moment, I dipped my head and brushed my lips over hers. Electricity sizzled between us, zinging through my body in a fiery path.

In an instant, what had started as almost a test—testing if the fire burned as hot as I remembered, testing if Daphne wanted this as fiercely as I did—shifted into something much more real. I brushed my lips over hers. When I heard a little catch in her throat and felt her hand slide up around my neck, with her fingers teasing in the ends of my hair, I stepped closer. This entire moment felt liquid, like warm honey dripping from a spoon. On an exhale, I angled her head to the side as I delved into her mouth with my tongue.

The second her tongue slid against mine, our kiss

became a mad dash. I heard my growl, and then I was pulling her flush against me as her tongue dueled with mine in silky, sensual strokes.

As if the gates holding me back had been blown to pieces, I fumbled to pull her closer. Daphne was pure octane poured on a fire already burning solely for her.

I felt the press of her nails as her hand slid down my back in a hurried stroke, and then her palm was warm on my skin when she pushed my shirt up.

When I tore my mouth roughly from hers and blazed a damp trail down her neck with my lips and teeth, she gasped, "Flynn!"

I was heedless of everything but Daphne and the need whipping through me. I shoved her T-shirt up with one hand, groaning aloud when my palm made contact with her silky soft skin. I cupped a breast roughly, lightly pinching her nipple and letting out a growl of satisfaction when it pebbled to a tight peak under my touch.

Pushing her shirt up farther, I brought my mouth over her nipple as I tugged her bra down, and her breast plumped up. I needed to touch her, to have her. Her hand gripped my hair as my mouth closed over her nipple roughly, too roughly. But I couldn't think; I couldn't slow this down.

Daphne was just as frantic as me. Her hands were busy yanking at the buttons on my jeans while I shoved her leggings down around her hips. I pushed her panties out of the way to discover her slick, hot, and ready. Her head fell into the crook of my neck, and I felt the warm gust of her breath across my collarbone as she shuddered when I sank two fingers into her channel.

I needed more. I needed *all* of her this time. She cried out when I drew my fingers away, but I lifted her in my arms, murmuring, "I have you. Just let me take care of you."

My mind was hazed with lust and need with an intense protectiveness tangling inside of that. Spinning around, I slid her hips on the counter and then yanked her leggings and panties free where they fell to the floor.

When I stepped between her legs, Daphne shimmied her hand into my open fly, stroking over my cock once through my boxers before she pushed them down, and it bounced free. Everything was a rush as our bodies communicated without words.

I need you.

Now.

Can't wait

Hurry.

Then my crown was at her slick entrance, and her legs were curling around my waist. The slow glide into her slick sheath was beyond intoxicating. Our heads bowed together as we breathed raggedly. Our hearts felt as if they were beating to their own metronome.

Chapter Seventeen

DAPHNE

I could hardly breathe through the storm of sensation as I clung to Flynn. The rush of him filling me was intense. It had been a while, and I was tight. When I gasped, he murmured right beside my ear, "Just wait. I'll take care of you."

I was restless and impatient, need nipping sharply at my heels. He held still and then pulled my hips closer to the edge of the counter, eliciting a raw moan when I felt the luscious stretch of him as he sank deeper into me.

With the shift of position, my legs loosened, and the angle created subtle friction exactly where I needed it. Flynn held me easily, one hand tangling in my hair as our heads bowed together. His other hand was wrapped around my hips, his palm holding me with ease.

I was awash in pleasure. I simply gave in, surrendering to the moment, into Flynn's strong hold in a way I'd never let go in my life. I was so accustomed to being strong, to holding myself together that the experience of letting go heightened every sensation.

Flynn's lips pressed against the side of my neck in a hot, open kiss. Every sensation spun into the rest. Again and again, he shifted back slightly and then buried himself inside me. All the while, I chased after my sweet release as the tension tightened to an almost unbearable pain inside.

I heard myself pleading, and then his whispered reply, "I have you here. Let go."

So I did. Everything pulled tight in my very center. It snapped, and pleasure spun like fiery pinwheels throughout my body as my channel clenched around him. I heard his ragged gasp as his mouth dragged along my neck in another open-mouthed kiss. I felt the lustrous heat of his release fill me and held on tight.

We stayed frozen like that for several moments. My heartbeat was rioting in my chest. I was sated, relaxed beyond all measure. As if my mind and heart knew something my body didn't, a sense of panic started to creep in, and I tensed.

Somehow, Flynn seemed to know precisely what I needed before I did. His hand loosened in my hair, and his palm slipped down my back in a soothing caress. "Princess, just relax."

So I did. I didn't know how long we stayed there with me seated ingloriously on the counter. Flynn eventually untangled himself, and we tidied our clothes.

I was almost in shock from the depth of intimacy that had passed between us. When I finally brought myself to look up at him, I offered, "I'm on the pill."

Flynn's eyes searched my face quietly. "I usually stop to think, but you kind of make me lose my mind."

I bit my lip, feeling my cheeks get hot. "It seems we do that to each other."

Flynn looked as if he wanted to say more, but I wasn't ready for more. I closed the distance between us and leaned up to press a kiss on his stubbled jawline. "Good night, Flynn," I whispered before turning and hurrying out of the kitchen.

It was only after I was halfway up the spiral staircase that I remembered I left some popovers in the oven. Returning to the kitchen, I found Flynn checking on them. He ended up helping me clean up without a word passing between us. Somehow, he knew I needed quiet.

I fell asleep a little bit later, wondering how Flynn understood me so well.

"Come again," I said, glancing in Diego's direction.

"I said it looks like you're pissing Mandy off," Diego commented, leaning back in his chair before taking a swallow from his beer.

I didn't even look in Mandy's direction. I occasionally spent time with Mandy, on a *very* casual, not often basis. I wouldn't even call it a friends with benefits arrangement. We were friendly, and there were occasional benefits.

I took a bite of my pizza and shrugged. "I doubt it. Plus, why would she be pissed off at me?"

Elias's brows hitched. "Because you're ignoring her. I'm not saying she has some sort of claim on you. But when you do see her, she usually gets what she wants from you. That's all."

"Tonight, she might as well be invisible," Diego added with a roll of his green eyes.

I glanced between my two friends and shrugged. "She's not invisible. I'm just not in the mood."

We were out for dinner at Diamond Creek Brewery. It was housed in an old plane hangar. The open space had been turned into a restaurant and brewery. The brewery part of the business was in the back with the stainless steel equipment partially visible behind a brick wall. In a touch of whimsy, there were model planes hanging from the ceiling. This place was popular with locals and tourists.

Every few weeks, we came here for food and drinks. The food was always good, and their beer selection was hard to beat. Gabriel and Grant had just left a few minutes ago to go play pool at Sally's Bar, another local favorite. Tucker was a few hours away, doing an overnight tourist trip in the Katmai area.

Diego ran a hand through his dark hair, casting me a sly grin. "I think I know why you're not interested."

Elias cleared his throat. "We all know why."

I kept my expression bland. "Do tell."

"You have it bad for Daphne," Elias countered swiftly.

"Your princess," Diego said with a wink.

I masked my irritation by taking a swallow of my beer. "Since when do you two pay attention to who I want?"

Diego shrugged easily. "Dude, we live to get under your skin. It's not easy. In fact, I don't think any woman has gotten under your skin since I've known you. Except for Daphne."

"Well, that would be because I don't have time. In case you missed the memo, I work all the time, and I happen to like it that way."

Elias looked over at me from across the table, his gaze sobering. "You do work all the time. I'm familiar with that tendency because I do too. We all like Daphne. She's awesome."

"And her food is fucking amazing," Diego said with

a vigorous nod. "Don't screw it up by getting cranky with her."

"Better yet, don't screw it up by fucking her and making things complicated," Elias commented.

My friends had no freaking clue how complicated things already were. It'd been bad enough when I was only a little obsessed with her before that night. After that, it had felt like a game of whack-a-mole in my brain as I tried to keep my thoughts of Daphne from breaking through every free moment.

After the other night in the kitchen? I was totally screwed.

Every second of that encounter was burned deeply into my mind and had imprinted her on every cell of my body. Throwing emotions into the mix was turning out to be insanely complicated for me.

"Can we lay off giving me shit about Daphne? The last thing I need is to screw up the situation with the best chef we've ever had." Avoidance was the only defense I had at the moment.

Diego nodded solemnly. "Exactly."

"Your mom seems to be enjoying herself," I commented to Elias, figuring that would take the focus off me.

Elias flashed a grin. "She is. She also noticed you have a thing for Daphne and thinks Daphne would be good for you."

I hung my head and groaned.

Diego took pity on me. "Aw, we'll leave ya alone for now."

"Hey, guys," a voice said.

Glancing to the side, I saw Jared Winters approaching the table. After a chorus of greetings from us, Jared looked toward me. "So are you going to take Trey up on his offer?"

"Think so," I replied. "I just need to hammer out the financials. I don't have enough cash to buy him out outright, so I need to talk to the bank."

Jared eyed me speculatively. "You can work it out. I wish I could fly planes. I'd take him up on it in a hot minute."

"Hey, man, we'll take you up in the air for your instruction hours," Diego offered with a quick grin.

Jared ran a charter boat business with his two brothers. While we flew through the skies, they did everything on the water. They often sent us customers, and we did the same in return.

Jared's green eyes twinkled with his chuckle. "Nah, man. I don't have time to learn something new. Don't forget I have a toddler to chase," he added.

Diego spoke first. "Toddlers either ruin people for more kids or not. What's your vote?"

Jared chuckled. "Good point. It was the sleepless nights that got to me when he was a baby."

"Well, there's always that," Diego replied with a grin.

Jared nodded. "Yup. Trust me, having a baby is harder than flying a plane, but I'd do it all over again. Anyway, I need to keep moving. Just here to pick up some takeout and a few growlers of beer."

"Catch you later," I said with a wave.

Jared's interruption got Diego and Elias off further discussion of Daphne. We chatted about this and that. Unfortunately—for me, at least—Daphne was never far from my thoughts. After I waved goodbye to them, since they rode here together, Mandy waylaid me in the parking lot.

"Flynn!" she called.

Glancing over my shoulder, I saw her crossing the parking lot, her footsteps crunching on the gravel.

I smiled, keeping my expression bland. Mandy stopped beside where I stood at the back of my truck.

"Hey."

I inclined my head. "Hey."

Mandy was gorgeous. She had rich chestnut hair and big blue eyes. She was tall and willowy and usually down for a good time with no strings attached.

That worked for me most of the time. It's just that I didn't even feel the slightest twinge of interest for her now. I wasn't comparing them because that wasn't fair. It's just that Daphne with her petite, curvy body and her flashing green eyes was the only thing that drew my interest these days. With Mandy standing in front of me, her eyes narrowed and curious, I actually tried to be interested.

I felt nothing, freaking nothing.

"I'm off for the night," she offered with just a hint of a question at the end.

"Good to see you, Mandy, but I've had a long day, and I'm tired. I have an early morning tomorrow." I was being entirely honest there.

Mandy's eyes searched my face. "I take it you're not interested."

I shook my head.

Mandy stared at me, her eyes narrowing slightly as she rested a hand on her hip. "You know, that's the first time you've turned me down."

Oh, fuck. She was not letting this go. "Mandy, don't take it personally."

Mandy rolled her eyes. "It *is* personal, Flynn."

Clearly, she *was* taking it personally. I wasn't sure what to make of her irritation with me. "Look, I thought we were clear on this. No expectations. I haven't seen you in months."

Mandy eyed me for a long beat before letting out

an annoyed huff. "It's not that I expect anything from you, but I thought we had something."

Apparently, Mandy was only easy to deal with as long as I gave her what she wanted. I spun my keys around my index finger as I looked at her. "I'm not sure what to say, Mandy." I really wasn't.

"Fuck you, Flynn."

"I'm sorry, Mandy."

She stalked away, anger radiating from her as she threw up her middle finger over her shoulder. So much for that. I genuinely hadn't meant to hurt Mandy. We'd never been serious. Hell, I'd maybe hung out with her three or four times over the past year. My life didn't leave room for much socializing. Apparently, her attitude was only easygoing if she got what she wanted. With a sigh, I climbed in my truck.

I drove home, trying to ignore the drumbeat of anticipation. I couldn't help but wonder if Daphne would be up late in the kitchen again.

It didn't slip my awareness that my very anticipation made my dismissal of Mandy bullshit. I was tired, and I did have an early morning tomorrow. Yet that didn't change the fact I wanted Daphne. I'd stay up all night for her.

Chapter Nineteen

DAPHNE

"Flynn! I told you I was at Sara's. I wasn't with Jonathon." Cat spun around with an irritated huff and stalked out of the kitchen.

I kept busy at the counter, where I was adding spices to a dip.

Nora's dry reply reached my ears. "You know she gets upset when you don't just check before giving her a hard time about something."

I didn't even need to look to know that Flynn most likely threw a withering glare in Nora's direction. "I know. I'll go call Sara's mom now. Parenting a sixteen-year-old isn't exactly easy," he muttered.

He walked away, going through the door that led into the private area where he and Cat lived. I looked up to see Nora looking worried where she stood by the table. She glanced up just as I did, meeting my eyes. "Those two." She gestured to where Flynn had just disappeared.

I shrugged lightly. "It's not easy being a teenager. I can't imagine it's easy for Flynn to be in charge since he's her brother."

Nora crossed the kitchen, sliding her hips onto a stool on the other side of the counter. "No, it's not. Flynn didn't sign up for this."

"I don't sense that he resents the responsibility at all," I offered. "Even people who did sign up to be parents don't usually enjoy dealing with their teenagers."

"Of course not. I just wish Flynn didn't work so much. It only adds to his stress."

I nodded and turned to check on something in the oven. I had a million and one questions about Flynn, but assuaging my curiosity by asking them would only create curiosity about why I was so curious. There was *way* too much curiosity going on.

"Flynn and Cat will be fine," I commented as I turned back to snag a baking pan. Setting it on the counter, I began to spoon the red pepper spinach dip into the pan.

"I know they'll be okay. Cat adores him. It's been good to have you here. Aside from the food, which is awesome by the way, Cat really likes you," Nora said.

I smiled. "I like her too. She's so funny. She wants nothing more than to fly planes like Flynn and Grant."

"I know. She also wants to have more freedom than Flynn gives her."

"Shocking," I returned dryly.

"She also wants to join the Air Force like Flynn. Needless to say, Flynn is totally against it. They've been arguing about it off and on for the past year."

My heart squeezed for both Cat and Flynn. "I can see why Cat would want to do what he did. But I can see why Flynn would be worried."

Nora nodded. "I get it too, so for now, I'm staying out of it. Plus, Flynn's just cranky lately. I wish he would find someone to lighten him up. But he refuses to consider it. He doesn't believe in love because of our mother and her shitty luck with men."

Okay, now my million and one questions ballooned to two million questions about Flynn. Saving me from my curiosity, Flynn opened the door at the back of the kitchen and came striding out with a dark expression. He said nothing to Nora and me as he strode by. Nora cast me a concerned look and pushed away from the counter to follow her brother.

A few minutes later, Cat came out. "Flynn's being an asshole," she announced.

I was putting dishes in the dishwasher and glanced over my shoulder. "He's gone now, so no need to make a scene about it."

"Ever since I forgot to tell him Jonathon would be at Sara's party last weekend, we've argued three times. Will you talk to him for me?"

Startled, I lowered my hands and turned to face her. "Definitely not."

"Daphne, please," Cat implored.

"Cat, there's no way I'm talking to your brother about this. It's definitely what I would call a family matter." I reached for a clean towel from the stack I kept on the counter beside the dishwasher.

"But Flynn likes you. He'll listen," Cat protested.

My mind flashed to exactly what we did on the kitchen counter a few nights prior. Since then, Flynn had reverted to his distant reserve with me and only called me princess once. I didn't think what happened here in the kitchen—which I prayed to every God possible that Cat didn't know about it—was what she meant about Flynn liking me.

"Hon," I said as I crossed the kitchen to her. "I

work here now, and Flynn has a habit of running his chefs off. I'd like to stay on good terms with him. I am absolutely positive trying to talk to him about anything you're arguing with him about isn't a good idea. Plus..." I paused and lifted a hand to lightly squeeze her shoulder. "You're sixteen. You're going to mess up in big ways and small ways. Just be patient."

Cat's blue eyes, so similar to Flynn's with that smoky rim, scrunched up as she wrinkled her nose and let out a dramatic sigh. "Why does everyone tell me to be patient? It feels like it will be forever before I'll be old enough to just do what I want."

Nora happened to return to the kitchen at that moment. Cat swung in her direction. "Even Daphne won't talk to Flynn." At that, she stormed off.

I met Nora's worried eyes and lifted my hands in the air before letting them fall. "Sorry. I didn't mean to upset her more. I just told her I wouldn't interfere between her and Flynn."

Nora sighed. "If she's gonna listen to anyone, it's you. She adores you, you know?"

"She does?"

Nora smiled. "She asks to go to town with you every chance she gets. She loves having you here. She doesn't warm up to people easily, so the fact that she wants to spend any time alone with you is a miracle. I think she sort of thinks of you like a mother."

I absorbed that startling observation quietly. "Want some fresh coffee?" I asked when Nora leaned her elbows on the counter.

"Yes, please."

Nora and I were sipping coffee a few minutes later when she commented, "It's not like any of us had the greatest role models for parents. That's why Cat looks up to you so much."

I thought of my own appearance-obsessed parents. "What do you mean? Y'all are so close."

Nora nodded. "We are. Our mom was great; it's just she didn't have good luck with men. Flynn's father never stuck around. We're close to Flynn now, but we weren't when we were younger. He was too much older. Our dad was an asshole," Nora said, her lips turning down. "He never stuck around, just came and went. He was really a jerk to Flynn because he hated that my mom had ever been with anybody else. Mind you, we probably have half siblings somewhere because that man couldn't keep it in his pants."

"Was he abusive?"

Nora drummed her fingertips on the table. "Not physically, if that's what you mean. Definitely emotionally with our mother. He jerked her chain all the time. When she got sick, he could hardly be bothered to be there for her. She inherited this property from her parents when they passed away. Lo and behold, he showed up then. They had started this resort way back when but never quite finished it. The one thing he did was construction, so he did a lot of the work on this place. As far as us kids, he was just a big ball of couldn't-be-bothered. With Flynn, he was kind of mean. Flynn had it out with him a few times before he died. Flynn is the closest thing any of us have to a father, but I'm not sure how he feels about being in that role. He's intensely loyal and protective, so I think it's been hard on him sometimes. He works his ass off for us. Cat looks up to him so much. That's why she wants to join the Air Force. She doesn't understand it worries him. If you didn't catch this detail yet, all the guys that fly here for us followed him here after they got out of the Air Force."

"I figured that out. I noticed they're all pretty tight."

"I just wish Flynn would let somebody take care of him the way he takes care of everybody else. Everybody comes before him."

Chapter Twenty

FLYNN

Cat gave me the silent treatment for the rest of the day. Fortunately, I had a few puddle jumper flights, so I was busy. Cat texted me later, asking permission to spend the night with her friend Sara. After confirming with Sara's mom, I let her go. When I returned that night, it was late. Again. This time, it was because I ended up doing engine checks on all of our planes.

I came by my workaholic label honestly. When I cut the engine to my truck and turned off my headlights, I didn't miss the fact that I could see two windows illuminated in the darkness. Those windows were in the kitchen.

The mere thought that Daphne might be awake sent electricity sizzling down my spine. I tried to tamp it down, but what I thought was intellectually smart and the right thing to do—avoid Daphne—had little force in the face of my burgeoning need for her.

I walked quietly into the side door, which led into a hallway that offered a back entrance to the private area where Cat and I stayed. I hung my jacket on one of the hooks on the wall and paused by the door that led into the kitchen when I heard a voice.

"Mom, I'm not coming home, and I can't believe you're even asking."

That was unmistakably Daphne's voice. She didn't have much of a Southern accent, but every now and then, it slipped through.

She went quiet, and I couldn't believe I was standing there eavesdropping. But then I couldn't believe much of anything I did when it came to Daphne. Rational didn't apply.

After another moment, when I presumed she was listening to her mother on the other end of the line, she said, "Brandon is dead. I know it would be convenient for you if I came back and made nice with Pete, but I won't. This isn't about business for me. If I ever wondered what I meant to you and Dad, I know I never was your priority. You just convinced me I was because I went along with everything you wanted. I'm not coming home. Brandon is dead, and I can't believe you're asking me to make nice with his father. Pete screwed around on me with someone who I thought was my friend. While Brandon was sick." Daphne's voice had a sharp edge with that last sentence.

Anger spun in a tight fist around my heart. I knew the details of what happened because Daphne had told Nora. Yet it still infuriated me to hear them spelled out in her voice.

There was another long silence, and then Daphne said, "I'm hanging up now. Goodbye."

I didn't realize my hand was on the doorknob until I felt myself gripping it tightly. I didn't know what Daphne was feeling, but I was fucking pissed off at her mother.

Her silence dragged out just long enough that I

almost convinced myself not to march into the kitchen. Until I heard her breath come out in a ragged sigh.

I was through the door in less than a second. I closed it quietly behind me to find Daphne with her hands resting on the counter, and her head bowed, and her shoulders shaking slightly.

"Daphne."

She spun around, her hand flying to her chest. Her green eyes were bright from her tears, and her cheeks damp. "Flynn. I didn't know you were here."

"I heard the last part of your conversation. I don't like your mother," I said flatly.

Daphne's eyes widened. She knuckled at her eyes with one fist and shrugged. "I don't really like her either," she said with a bitter laugh.

"Just so you know, I don't usually eavesdrop."

She regarded me quietly. "No?" Her lips twitched slightly.

"No. Are you done for the night?"

I finally broke my gaze from hers and scanned the kitchen. Everything was turned off and put away. Daphne's apron lay in a rumple on the counter with a towel beside it.

When my eyes returned to her, she nodded. "I was just about to go upstairs, but I was thinking about having a glass of wine first. It's been a *day*."

"Come with me." Striding to her, I lifted the towel and her apron off the counter and tossed them in the laundry bin beside the dishwasher. Catching her hand in mine, I drew her toward the door.

She stopped, tugging on my hand. "I can't go in there," she whispered. "Cat's in there, and she should be in bed if she's not already."

"Cat's spending the night with a friend. And there's no need to whisper."

Daphne's mouth dropped into a pretty little O, and it was all I could do not to kiss her. "Come with me," I repeated. "I have something for you."

Daphne followed me. When I first came back from the military to take care of Grant, Nora, and Cat, this section was unfinished. I'd immediately completed this part of the resort first so we had somewhere comfortable to live.

The main area was a combined living room and kitchen. I toed my shoes off, and Daphne followed suit. She was wearing an oversized T-shirt tied in a knot at her waist over a pair of leggings. She looked up at me as if waiting for me to tell her where to go.

"Be right there," I said as I gestured toward the sectional sofa that took up most of the space in the living room.

Crossing into the kitchen, I fetched two bottles of hard cider from Diamond Creek Brewery. Returning to the living room, I set the bottles on the table. Daphne was seated with her hips on the edge of the sofa, and her hands clasped over her knees. She had that tidy, princess vibe going strong. I wanted to kiss her senseless and mess her hair up.

"Did you try some of this when you went to the lodge restaurant with Nora?" I asked as I opened the bottles.

Daphne shook her head. "I had wine. What's this?"

"Delia's cider. It's really good. She started bottling it and selling it through the brewery about a year ago."

Daphne curled her hand around a bottle and lifted it, leaning forward to sniff. "It smells crisp."

I took a sip and commented, "I don't care how it smells; it's delicious."

Daphne took a swallow, her lips stretching in a slow smile. "It's absolutely delicious. Cider isn't really a thing in the South, you know."

"I don't actually know because I've never been to the South. Since apple trees grow where it's colder, it makes more sense that it's popular where it snows."

Daphne took another sip. She let out a low moan as she lowered the bottle to the coffee table. *Fuck me.* Daphne and food and drinks were dangerous. She was always exclaiming over flavors and smells. It was a good thing I was too busy to be in the kitchen often, except when I scarfed down food.

"You can relax, you know," I said, patting the back of the couch.

Daphne rolled her eyes as she shimmied her hips back into the cushions. Curling her knees up to her chest, she wrapped one arm around them. I didn't like the vulnerability flickering in her eyes. As strong as she was, her gaze had an almost bruised quality tonight. Knowing what she'd been through, it amazed me how well she held it together most of the time.

"How was your day?" she asked politely.

I took another swallow of my cider before setting it down. She leaned forward to reach for her bottle, but I beat her to it and handed it over.

Her knees slid down until she was sitting cross-legged with her hands curled around the bottle of cider.

She took another swallow as I replied, "Busy."

"Your days are always busy, Flynn. Nora thinks you work too much and worries about you."

I chuckled. "I know she does. You're the pot, and I'm the kettle. I think you work too much ever since I discovered your habit of staying up late and baking."

She held my gaze solemnly and took another

swallow of her cider. She was making quick work of it. "That stuff is strong," I murmured.

"I need strong tonight."

"Tell me why you don't want to go home."

Daphne took two more swallows before lowering her bottle again. "Nora told you everything, huh?"

"I think so."

"Well, things are messy because my ex and his family are my father's business partners. He's next in line at my father's company as the CFO. My parents would like me to make nice and smooth things over. Appearances are very important to them. I didn't realize how little appearances mattered until Brandon died."

Daphne's words came out calm and measured with little emotion. It was almost as if she'd practiced saying this.

I didn't realize I'd shifted closer to her and reached for her until my palm was sliding down her arm. She released one of her hands from the bottle, allowing me to curl mine around hers.

"You're cold."

She shrugged. "I'm cold most of the time. It's a downside to being small."

"Not a fan of your mother," I commented.

Daphne regarded me quietly and took another sip of her cider. "You don't need to be angry on my behalf." She lifted her chin slightly as she spoke, a surefire way to rev the engine of my need for her.

"I know you can take care of yourself, Daphne, but that doesn't mean I can't be protective. There's nothing you can do about it."

"I'm pretty sure there's nothing I can do about anything you think or anyone else for that matter." She took another gulp of her cider, draining the bottle before leaning forward to set it on the coffee table. When she leaned back, I scooped her up and pulled her onto my lap.

Chapter Twenty-One

FLYNN

"Come here," I murmured as I dipped my head and pressed an open-mouthed kiss on the side of her neck. She tasted like sugar with a hint of salt tonight.

"That wasn't really a request, not when you pulled me onto your lap," she said with a throaty giggle.

Lifting my head, I nodded as I smoothed her hair away from her face. "I suppose it wasn't. Tell me what you were baking tonight before I got back."

"Croissants."

Leaning forward, I trailed the tip of my nose along her jawline. "Is that butter I smell, then?"

She giggled again, and my cock swelled to an ache. "Maybe."

That single word came out breathy as I nipped lightly on her earlobe. I lifted a hand to tug the elastic out of her hair.

"What are you doing, Flynn?" she asked. A little gasp escaped when I cupped a breast and dragged my thumb across the ruched peak of her nipple.

"Tasting you," I murmured into her neck. I

dragged my tongue along the soft skin there before lightly scraping it with my teeth.

Daphne shivered in my arms. I felt her hand curl over my shoulder and slide down. "No fair," she gasped when I pinched her nipple.

"What's not fair, princess?"

Daphne went still in my lap, and I lifted my head. She searched my face before commenting, "That's only the second time you've called me princess since the other night."

My heart thrashed in my chest. Of course, she noticed. Daphne paid attention to everything. You see, I'd made a conscious effort not to call her by that endearment. It was some sort of stupid attempt to convince myself I didn't have it this bad for her.

"How come?" she added.

"You tell me what's not fair first," I returned while my heart kicked away.

Her cheeks went pink, and I had to hold myself still to keep from kissing her. She trailed her fingers across my chest. "You're too sexy. I bet you don't even work out."

I shook my head slowly. "Princess, my life is a workout."

She stared at me and lifted her chin slightly, almost as if she were daring me to avoid her question. My heart gave a tricky twist. I knew exactly why I hadn't called her princess. It's just I didn't want to discuss it directly. But then I'd be a coward. All the while, Daphne sat here, a lush bundle in my lap.

"To be honest, you drive me a little crazy, and I've been trying to stay sane around you."

Daphne blinked and bit the corner of her lip. The corner I wanted to kiss. So I leaned forward and dropped a kiss on one corner of her mouth and then the other.

"I drive you crazy?" she asked in her husky voice.

"Uh-huh." I felt my lips kick up into a slow smile. "I don't like admitting it, but it's true."

"Well, that's handy. Because you drive me crazy, and I thought you were gonna start ignoring me again."

"Again?" I countered.

Her cheeks flushed a deeper shade of pink. "Yeah. After the night up at that guy's place." She gestured vaguely in a direction, which happened to be the opposite of where Henry's hunting lodge was.

Sliding an arm around her hips, I pulled Daphne a little closer. It was all I could do not to ravage her right then and there, considering the unholy temptation.

"I know I can be cranky, but it so happens I like you, princess."

I hadn't planned it this way. Hell, I hadn't planned anything with Daphne. But somehow, this felt intimate. I was unveiling secrets I didn't even let myself think about, much less feel like a foolish boy about a girl.

Daphne tucked her head into my shoulder and wiggled her bottom slightly, the little minx. "It so happens I like you too, Flynn."

She lifted her head, bringing her hand to trace along my stubbled jawline. Then we were kissing, kisses that went on and on and on. She rose, straddling my lap. When she settled her hips down with a little hum, teasing me, I growled and broke my lips free from hers.

"You're too much," I muttered between breaths.

Daphne gave me a wicked smile before shimmying

back and reaching between us to my fly. She moved fast. In another second, her hand was curling around my hard, hot length. She rubbed over the tip of my cock, where a drop of pre-cum was leaking out. When she lifted her thumb and licked it, it was the hottest thing I'd ever seen.

In another second, she was kneeling and leaning forward to taste me, a subtle swipe across the tip, and then a swirl as she sucked the crown into her mouth. When she angled her head sideways and cast a hot look at me, I almost came right then.

"Princess—" A groan broke free.

Immediately following that, she took me in her mouth, her tongue gliding along the underside of my cock. Over the next few minutes, I learned Daphne was entirely willing to torture me. She teased me by sucking me deep and drawing back, almost letting me tumble into my release but never quite letting me. She slid up and swirled her tongue around the head of my cock. Next, she cupped the base lightly in her fist.

Somewhere in there, I scrambled for control as hot licks of electricity tightened at my balls. "Daphne," I gasped, gripping her hair. If it stung, she didn't care. She laughed slyly before drawing me into the warm heat of her mouth again.

This time, I tugged maybe too hard on her hair, and she lifted her head.

"Yes?"

She was all sassy and so fucking sexy that I was pretty sure she'd ruined me forever. No other woman could ever make me this insane. She'd crashed into me like an asteroid, obliterating any past memories of passion.

"I need to be inside you," I bit out.

Blessedly, she answered my plea and rose to her

feet. I was treated to a quick striptease when she flung her T-shirt off and shimmied out of her leggings. Her bra followed as I reached between her thighs, cupping my palm over her mound. The silk of her panties was soaked.

She was standing between my knees now, and when I looked up, her breasts were rising and falling with her short pants. Her nipples were pebbled tight, and I couldn't resist leaning forward to drag my tongue around one and suck it in. Her fingers speared in my hair as I moved to the other. I teased my knuckle lightly over that silk where I could feel her swollen clit underneath.

I loved her body. Leaning my head back, I took in her tidy form. She was petite, and her breasts were just perfect, a handful. Her ass was sweet. The lush curve of one cheek dented under my fingers as I gave it a squeeze. She gasped when I brought my hand between her thighs again, still just teasing her over the silk.

"Flynn," she breathed, a little whimper escaping.

"Yes?" I mirrored her earlier teasing.

"I need you inside me." Her lashes swept up, and she pinned me with her dark gaze.

Just because I couldn't resist, I pushed the silk out of the way and teased my fingers in her slick folds. I felt her pussy ripple at her entrance. I stood quickly.

Daphne gave me another saucy look. "You have too many clothes on."

With a low chuckle, I tossed my T-shirt aside and kicked off my jeans and boxers. She turned and shimmied out of her underwear. I was greeted by the sight of her bottom, heart-shaped and plump. I slid a hand over one cheek and gave it a light slap. When she looked over her shoulder at me, I knew exactly what I wanted.

"Bend over."

I was gratified when Daphne complied immediately. In another second, her hands were curling over the back of the couch, and I was sliding one hand over her hip as I gripped the other. Fisting my cock, I dragged it through her folds.

She made this little sound, something between a whimper and a moan. In one swift surge, I filled her and slid a palm up her spine to lightly grip her hair.

With Daphne rocking her hips back into me and her channel slick and tight around me, I filled her again and again and again. My release was so close; it was all I could do to hold back. Hot lightning sizzled up my spine as she met me stroke for stroke.

Releasing her hair, I slipped my hand around and found her hot button of need swollen when I teased my fingers around it. She cried out roughly, her hips bucking against me as her channel spasmed tightly and pulled my release from me.

There was a roar through my entire body as everything went tight before my release snapped free. When my awareness flickered back on, my head was hanging down while I gasped for breath and shudders wracked my body.

I was gripping Daphne's hip too tightly, so I slowly released it and smoothed my palm over her skin. I withdrew reluctantly and lifted her in my arms because I needed to stay close to her.

Daphne lifted her arm, her fingers teasing at the base of my neck in my hair. "Where are we going?" Her voice was a little hoarse.

"Shower," I murmured before dipping my head and pressing an open-mouthed kiss on the side of her neck. I loved that I could feel the goose bumps rise on her skin as I walked through my bedroom and into the only area of privacy I ever had in my life these days, my personal bathroom.

When I nudged the light switch with my elbow, Daphne lifted her head and looked around. "Oh, this isn't the bathroom you took me to before."

"Nope. This is my bathroom." I kept her in my arms all the way across the room to the shower as I reached in with one arm and turned it on.

"You can put me down, you know," she said with a little laugh.

That was the crazy thing. Usually, I treated sex with as much enthusiasm as I did eating. Oh, I liked it just fine, but it was a basic need. Once the need was assuaged, I was all set.

But with Daphne, I wanted more. In fact, I could've gone another round right then, but more than that, I wanted to fall asleep with her.

"In a sec." I stepped in the shower and eased her down under the steaming water.

Chapter Twenty-Two

DAPHNE

One moment blurred into the next with Flynn. I found myself in the shower with him. He was quick and efficient at soaping himself. Before I knew it, he was sliding his hands over me and lifting me against the tiled wall as he filled me again.

Being with Flynn was a surfeit of pleasure. He brought me to another climax in a matter of seconds with his fingers. Then he stroked in and out of me as the water rained down around us. My next climax rolled through me in slow waves of intense pleasure.

After that experience—startling in its intimacy and not what I expected—he wrapped me in one of the fluffy robes they had here at the resort. We lounged on his bed, eating cheese. He said he craved it, so I fetched some from the darkened kitchen. I also learned he loved *Star Trek*. Since I was a huge fan and it was a guilty pleasure, that was awesome.

I also learned he loved the home improvement shows. That was another secret pleasure of mine. I didn't realize I'd fallen asleep propped up against the pillows until I felt the covers coming over me, cool against my skin. Flynn must've peeled off my robe because I was naked.

Goose bumps chased over my skin, and I whispered, "When is Cat coming home?"

"Not until tomorrow afternoon." His voice was low in the darkness. He curled up behind me and pulled me into his strong, muscled body.

As I drifted into sleep, I had a moment of startling recollection. My awful phone call with my mother. I'd forgotten it entirely. My heart gave an achy thump because I missed my little boy. But I was okay. Actually, I was more than okay. I felt warm and safe and sated beyond measure.

Somehow, Flynn knew precisely what I needed in order to forget. Because sometimes I truly did just need to escape from the weight of that grief. Considering that Flynn's magic fingers and lips and tongue and body could make me forget everything but him and the sensations spiraling through me, he was the perfect escape.

I wouldn't fall in love. I couldn't. I genuinely didn't believe I had the capacity. So, I would enjoy this for just what it was.

I fell into a dreamless sleep, more relaxed than I'd been in perhaps forever. Even before my life exploded into pieces, I was only scraping the surface. I didn't think about it much, but I'd known there was more to be had. I used to lay awake at night worrying about all the things I hadn't gotten done in my restaurant and in my family's business. Then I traded those worries for the cold, bracing fear of facing Brandon's almost certain death. Then I survived his actual death and the brutal betrayal of my husband and my friend and my family.

Here in Alaska, wrapped in Flynn's strong arms, I

could forget all that. When the worst has already happened, there was nothing else to worry about.

———

In the weeks that followed, Flynn and I settled into a routine. It involved him sneaking into my room every night, except for the ones when Cat spent the night out with friends. Those were about once a week. She'd explained to me she lived too far from town to do the fun stuff, so she usually spent the night with her friends there.

Flynn and I had what I figured had to be one of those once-in-a-lifetime types of chemistry. Sex was just *easy* with us. It was always fiery hot and so good it almost hurt. In those dark hours of our nights, there was no judgment and total freedom.

I was cleaning up in the kitchen after lunch one day when my phone rang.

"Hello," I said, answering without checking the number.

"Daphne, I need a ride," Cat said urgently.

She sniffled, and I suspected she was crying. My stomach clenched with worry. I was alone in the kitchen and looked around as if somehow someone would appear and tell me what to do. It was early afternoon, the time when everyone was usually gone. Flynn was likely in a plane, along with Grant, and Nora was taking a group on a hike.

"Cat, where are you? Aren't you at school?"

She sniffled again, and a little sob escaped. "I'm supposed to be." There was a long, heavy pause. "But I'm not. Can you please just come get me?"

"Cat, hon, I don't know if that's okay with Flynn."

I wanted to say yes—desperately—but I wasn't sure what to do.

Cat's gulping breath came through the phone loudly. I didn't know what happened, but I knew when a teenage girl was teetering on too upset to deal. I'd been one once and recalled clearly just how hard that time of life could be.

"I know, but I can't call Flynn. He's across the bay today. Every morning, he texts me his flight schedule so I'll know." My heart squeezed. Of course, he did. Flynn would want Cat to know where he was. "He won't be landing until after five thirty. Nora's on that hike, and Grant's flying today. Please, Daphne," Cat implored.

I didn't hesitate. "Of course. Tell me where you are, and I'll be there as soon as I can."

Cat quickly relayed the address, and I hesitated to even hang up the phone. "Are you going to be okay until I get there?" I asked. I had lowered my phone to put her on speaker while I entered the address in a map app. It was a half an hour drive.

"Yes. Just hurry."

With worry spinning tightly in my chest, I drove as fast as I could down the gravel road until I hit the highway. The pavement made me feel more confident about my driving, and I zoomed into town. Unfortunately, the cell reception sucked for most of the drive, but it improved as soon as I got closer to Diamond Creek.

Pulling up in front of a small house, I glanced at the clock on my dashboard. Cat should definitely be in school, and she wasn't. Instead, she was here. Before I even had a chance to get out, she came flying out the front door of the house.

In another moment, she was clambering into my

SUV, the rental I still had even though I rarely used it. I had so many questions, but I took one look at her face, and all I wanted to do was hug her. That would have to wait.

"Buckle up," I said as I started the engine again.

Cat did as I said, and I rolled to the end of the driveway and turned back onto the road. "Are you okay?" I finally asked between her occasional sniffles.

"Not really," she finally said.

"Mind telling me why you're not in school? You might as well get this over with and tell me because you're gonna have to do it with Flynn later," I offered gently.

I felt Cat looking at me, and I glanced sideways. "What?"

"I was hoping maybe you wouldn't tell Flynn," she muttered as she looked away to stare out the window.

"Cat, I can't do that," I said firmly. "What happened?"

I could see a tear roll down her cheek when I glanced over again even though she was studiously looking out the window. Reaching into the console between the seats, I pulled out a packet of tissues and silently handed them to her.

She blew her nose noisily and then let out a gusty sigh. "You know that guy I'm kind of seeing?"

"I believe I heard Nora teasing you a little the other day. Is this the same guy Flynn wouldn't let you go out on the boat with? Jonathon?"

"Yeah. I skipped class with him, and he took me to his dad's house. He wanted to have sex, and I said no. He called me a tease." All of this came out between sniffles.

"Cat, I'm sorry. Boys can be jerks sometimes. You're not a tease."

She sniffled again. "He's probably already posted about it somewhere. I hate that shit."

"I'm with you there. Social media isn't helpful with things like this. Do you still like him?" I asked gently.

"I don't know. I'm just mad."

"Well, don't beat yourself up if you kind of do," I said carefully. "Sometimes, people do shitty things, and then we try to please them anyway."

"I know. He's an asshole."

"Welcome to life," I said wryly. "People can be really shitty and not just guys."

"Really?" Cat asked.

I briefly glanced her way and nodded. "Absolutely. I've misjudged people myself. Trust me, you can't avoid it. I'm really proud of you for saying no. Even if he's an asshole about it, at least he didn't push you."

Cat let out a dramatic sigh, followed by a rough laugh. "I told him I'd kick him in the balls. I would too."

"Good for you," I said. She was less distressed now that she was away from the situation.

We rode in silence for a bit until I turned onto the road that would take us home. "Maybe we should talk about how you're going to tell Flynn."

Cat leaned her head against the seat and let out a groan. "He's going to be so pissed. I can't talk you into covering for me?"

I looked her way briefly and shook my head. "No. I can't do that. You skipped school, so for all we know, the school might've already called him. I understand why you don't want him to know, but I can't lie about this. I picked you up."

Cat was quiet until right before we pulled up to park in front of the resort. "Fine. I'll tell him. But I'm not gonna tell him about the whole thing."

"Okay, tell him what you want. Just know that if he asks me about it, I'll tell him you called, and I will tell him where I picked you up."

Cat looked at me with her eyes red from crying. "Fine."

Chapter Twenty-Three

FLYNN

I knocked on Cat's bedroom door and waited. Total silence greeted me.

"Cat," I called through the door. "The principal left me a message this afternoon while I was flying. I know you skipped your afternoon classes and missed the bus home. Please just come talk to me and tell me what's going on."

I leaned a hand on the doorframe above my head. Parenting wasn't easy. Plus, I wasn't technically Cat's parent. It had been hard enough with Nora. Grant had been eighteen when our mother died. He was far too mature for his years, having been the de facto parent to both Nora and Cat while their father was hardly around before he passed away, and then while our mom was sick.

It certainly wasn't fair to Grant, but he'd made my job easier. He'd actually been able to relax for once when I came home. Nora had been an epically cranky teen and furious with grief. I'd been so relieved when she settled down.

Now, Cat was giving me a run for my money. To my

knowledge, she'd never skipped classes before. She'd sure as hell never missed the bus. The bus didn't come all the way out to where we were, but it dropped her off at a rendezvous point where a rotation of parents picked up the various kids who lived out here. Nora usually picked up Cat for me.

I wasn't panicking right now because I knew she was home. Daphne texted me to let me know she'd picked her up when Cat requested.

"Come on, Cat. You're gonna have to come out of your room at some point."

I heard footsteps stop on the other side of the door and waited. "I'm fine, and I'm sorry."

Oh fuck, she sounded like she'd been crying. Cat had been the toughest kid when she was little. These days, she was all kinds of emotional, and I never knew how to handle it.

"Just talk to Daphne. She'll tell you what happened."

"Cat, come on. I'd rather hear it from you."

"I'm tired, and I'm embarrassed. Can we talk tomorrow?"

I had no idea. Was I supposed to follow through with some kind of consequence because she skipped classes today? Or was I supposed to give her a break until tomorrow because my heart was already breaking for whatever she was upset about?

I was a total softie. "Okay. Promise we'll talk tomorrow morning before you go to school?"

"Promise."

Even her voice was hoarse, and the crack in my heart widened. When I heard her footsteps moving away, muffled by the carpet, I let my hand fall from the door and turned, leaning against the wall. I needed to talk to Daphne. I wanted to see her anyway.

Because I couldn't stay away from her. I was in over my head with a petite princess who was everything I never thought. She should've been lost in Alaska. Maybe she was fresh and green to dealing with the way life was here, but she never hesitated. She lifted that chin and twitched her princess nose and tried. Every time I saw her, she was like a ray of sunshine breaking through the clouds.

Daphne had fucking ruined me for any other woman. When I found myself seeking her out, night after night after dark fell and Cat was asleep, I knew it was stupid. I even worried about what I would do if Daphne decided to go back to Atlanta. We even talked. *Talked*.

Her unvarnished honesty about what happened in her marriage somehow made it easier. She didn't try to hide anything, and she didn't seem to have any expectations of me. All the while, I found myself wanting her to have everything because she deserved that. Life had already been so unfair to her. It felt like it should be as smooth as glass now, or so I thought. I wanted her to want this life here. With me.

No one could laugh harder at that than me. I'd lost my fucking mind over her.

I glanced down at my watch. Dinner would just be finishing. I couldn't exactly storm the kitchen now and expect Daphne to chat. I could eat, though. My stomach growled as if in agreement. I hadn't actually had a bite since this morning when I left with a warm orange zest scone tucked in my pocket as I was running late. Of course, it was one of Daphne's scones and pure heaven.

I found Daphne at the sink a few minutes later, elbow deep in hot water as she scrubbed at something. An auburn curl was falling over her cheek. Conveniently, no one else was around. I crossed to her and brushed that curl away, giving in to the urge to drop a kiss right behind her ear.

"Flynn!" she whispered. Rather loudly, I might add.

"Yeah, Flynn," Elias drawled.

Turning, I found him standing in the doorway that led to the main area. *Oh, fuck.* When I looked back toward Daphne, her cheeks were bright pink, but she was seriously focused on whatever she was scrubbing.

I crossed over to Elias as he walked into the kitchen. "Please don't make this a public announce-ment," I said. Considering Daphne knew he was here and knew what he'd just witnessed, I didn't try to keep my voice low.

Elias chuckled. "No worries, man." He clapped me on the shoulder. "Everyone suspects it anyway."

He walked over toward Daphne, resting his hip against the counter. "Don't have a heart attack or worry about this. We all think you're the best thing that ever happened to Flynn."

Daphne looked up at him, uncertainty flickering in her gaze. Then she shrugged and rolled her eyes. "Whatever. Not much to do now."

Elias looked back toward me. Daphne kept on scrubbing. "Just checking in. I heard from Nora that you might need to do damage control with Cat. Want me to take that overnight trip tomorrow?"

I ran a hand through my hair with a sigh. "That would be great."

"You got it. Catch you later." He pushed away from the counter and started to walk out of the kitchen. He paused and glanced back toward Daphne. "Daphne?" She looked up again and finally drew her hands out of the sink. "Really, don't worry about it. You're awesome."

"Damn, that's high praise from you, dude," I teased.

He arched a brow. "Well, she is awesome, and her food is definitely the best."

With that, he departed with a wave over his shoulder. I guessed Nora had shared with a few of the others what happened to Daphne. The guys were all protective of her, and that was cool with me. Daphne could use it.

I returned to where she was drying her hands on a towel. "Sorry about that."

She lowered a hand and dipped it back in the sink to pull the drain out. Shrugging lightly, she looked at me. "It's okay. You seemed to want to keep things private, so I assumed..." Her words trailed off.

I got the sense she had an idea about me that I didn't like all that much. Her cheeks went pink, and I could see her chewing the inside of her cheek, something she did when she was nervous.

"You assumed what?" I pressed.

Daphne cleared her throat and lifted her chin before waving a hand vaguely in the air. "It's not like I thought we were, I don't know, a thing." She wound her arms around her waist. "But I figured you'd be embarrassed if anyone knew about us."

"Embarrassed?" I asked, legitimately confused.

"Yeah. I know I'm not your type. I don't mind that you call me princess, but I kind of get that the nickname was originally not complimentary."

I gave my head a shake. "You thought I'd be embarrassed about you?"

Daphne tightened her arms around her waist. "I mean, I understood that with Cat you didn't want it to be weird, but yeah, I guess I did. Why are you staring at me like I'm crazy?"

"Because that's crazy. I'm crazy about you. Yes, I have to think about Cat, but I guess I just figured you wanted to keep things private. Apparently, now I need to make it abundantly clear to everyone that I have it fucking bad for you."

Daphne was still chewing the inside of her cheek, so I stepped closer. I reached for one of her hands and unwound it from her waist, and then the other before pulling her into my arms. "Let me clarify. I am seriously crazy about you. I'm not embarrassed about you. I'd rather not have Cat subject to what goes on between us because the walls are thin, but that's really all I care about."

"Oh," Daphne said softly after a long pause.

"That's all I get?" I teased with my heart kicking against my ribs. Because yeah, against all reason, I had it *way* bad for her.

She laughed and tucked her forehead against my chest. "Maybe I have it bad for you too. But it doesn't seem like either one of us is in a place to take any of this seriously."

She lifted her head then. I had to swallow my words because I wanted to tell her we totally could. I needed to save that for later when I could think.

Just then, another voice reached us. "Yes!"

Turning, I saw Nora standing in the door to the back hallway with a fist lifted in the air.

"Do you mind?" I asked, giving her a pointed look.

"Sorry," she said quickly with an apologetic smile. "I thought this might be happening, and now I know."

"Later, Nora."

"Just letting you know I'm taking Cat with me. She'll spend the night at my place, okay?"

"Perfect. I don't think she wants to talk to me

tonight," I called in return. "Mind keeping this to yourself for now until I have a chance to talk to her?"

"Of course not," Nora said with a way too satisfied smile.

Daphne waved at her from the shelter of my arms, and Nora blessedly left, firmly closing the door behind her. "It's not very late, in case you didn't notice, so we're gonna get interrupted again," Daphne commented.

"I'll check on things out front and help you clean up, and then we can have some privacy in my place."

I was about to kiss her when Diego came walking in from the other side of the kitchen. He flashed us an amused grin, but he didn't say anything. Daphne stepped out of my arms and got to work.

While Daphne continued cleaning the kitchen, I made my usual evening loop through the resort. Diego snagged a beer and found me out front where I was putting away some rental gear that we kept on-site for guests.

He leaned his shoulder against the wall in the entryway. "So...Daphne?"

I closed the door to the massive closet and looked over. "Yes, Daphne. Go ahead and share your opinion," I offered with a sigh as I gestured toward him.

Diego chuckled and took a swallow from his beer. Lowering it, he eyed me speculatively. "I think it's a good thing. Just don't break her heart."

That comment was a quick slice right to my heart. I started to shake my head, but he continued, "I know you don't think it's serious, and I doubt she does. I'm just saying you've both been through a lot. Be smart."

At that, Diego turned and left. I returned to the kitchen to find Daphne sliding a rack of dishes into the dishwasher. She closed it and tapped the button to start it just as I reached her.

"Are you already finished? I was going to help."

"I know. But it's all done."

"Come on," I said, catching one of her hands in mine.

A few minutes later, Daphne was curled up on the couch with her feet tucked under her knees as she looked at me. "Cat told you to ask me?"

I gave a quick nod. "Yeah. I appreciate you letting me know right away that you went to pick her up. I got your text before I played the message from the principal who said Cat had skipped afternoon classes and missed the bus, so I didn't freak out since I knew you picked her up."

Daphne wrinkled her nose, her hand curling around the edge of a soft throw blanket. She rubbed it between her fingers. "I really didn't know what to do. I knew you were in the air, along with Grant, and Nora was out on the hike. I hope you know I wouldn't have gone to pick her up without talking to you first if there'd been any way for me to get ahold of you."

"I know. You don't need to worry about that. I'm glad you were here. Just tell me what the hell happened."

Daphne took a breath. "Well, she called, and I could tell she was crying—" She paused when I winced. "What?"

"I could tell she'd been crying when I talked to her through her bedroom door earlier. I'm guessing she cried all afternoon."

Daphne angled her head to the side, her eyes softening when she looked at me. "She stopped crying on the drive home, I promise. She's sixteen. Sometimes there's plenty of crying. Anyway, when I went to get her, she was at Jonathon's dad's house."

"What?" I asked, my tone coming out harsher than I intended.

Daphne narrowed her eyes and pursed her lips. "I bet you snuck girls into your house when you were sixteen."

I rolled my eyes. "Not really, but I would've if I could've. What else happened?"

"I'd really rather Cat tell you the rest."

"I know, but she told me to ask you."

A part of me was frustrated, but I appreciated Daphne trying to let Cat tell her story. Cat was safe, so that was enough.

Daphne wrinkled her nose again. "Here's all I'm gonna say. She's fine. He tried to push the boundaries, and she said no. It didn't go well."

"I'm gonna fucking kill him."

"You're not gonna kill anybody. I'm pretty sure she's moving on from this guy, so just leave it alone."

"That fucking jerk."

"Flynn, let it rest for now. Get the details from Cat when you talk to her tomorrow. She's safe, and she's fine."

I groaned. Taking a deep breath, I rested my elbows on my knees, dropping my face into my hands. "I don't know what to do with her. I suck at this parenting gig."

Daphne shifted closer, and then her hand slid down my back. "Grant and Nora are doing great, and so is Cat."

I lifted my head to look at Daphne. "Yeah, but Grant was eighteen when I came home to take care of them, and Nora was sixteen. I've been trying to be Cat's brother and father since she was nine. She's so stubborn and strong-willed. Like tonight, was I supposed to force her to talk to me? And I feel like she needs a consequence for skipping class."

"Sure, but I don't think you had to do it tonight. She's safe, and that's the most important part."

"Just so you know, you have my permission to pick Cat up at any time and any place whenever she calls. It doesn't matter where I am or what I'm doing. Even if she asks you not to tell me, just go get her. I want her safe."

Daphne held my gaze quietly as an intimacy flourished in the air around us. I trusted her implicitly. I knew if anyone needed her, she'd do whatever was necessary. She might be small, and she might look like a princess, but she had nerves of steel.

And she was fierce—so, so fierce.

I felt her hand slide in a circle on my back. "Good to know," she finally said, her voice soft.

Before I thought about it any further, I angled toward Daphne. Lifting a hand, I reached for the elastic holding her hair up. Her hair tumbled loose around her shoulders. I cupped her cheek, sliding my thumb across her plump bottom lip.

The feel of Flynn's thumb sliding across my lip and the way he cupped my cheek had my breath coming in shallow pants while my pulse skittered madly. I kept thinking that the more I was with Flynn—physically, that was—the intensity would start to lighten.

As if somehow the novelty of this fiercely erotic and intimate connection with him would wear off. If anything, it seemed to keep growing in depth. We had a once-in-a-lifetime kind of chemistry. I expected it to stay just that—physical and purely sexual.

Instead, with every moment I spent with him, my emotions were rising to the surface and breaking free, regardless of what I thought about it. After everything that happened, my grief was the only thing that elicited emotion for so long. Everything else had been buried after my life exploded. Now, I'd made it to the other side of my grief, and the glacier locked around my heart was melting.

Flynn traced his thumb around my lips in a sensual tease before his hand slid down the side of my neck, coming to rest between my breasts. My heart lunged as if it recognized his singular touch. I suppose it did.

His eyes searched mine, the blue darkening so much it faded into the charcoal rim. "I can't believe you thought I was embarrassed about you." His words came out soft and raspy, always low when it was just us. His voice alone could set me alight with sparks.

I tried to take a breath, but I didn't get much air and felt a little frantic. It was always like this when I was physically close to him. Any proximity to his potent force was hard to withstand.

I swallowed, my breath hitching when I began to speak. "I didn't know. I thought, at first, it was because of Cat. But you kind of keep your distance when anyone's around."

Flynn's lips kicked up, and my insides felt ticklish. I knew he could feel the wild beat of my heart under his palm.

"That's just because I'm trying not to tackle you every time I see you," he murmured, tugging me onto his lap.

Flynn's lap was my favorite place to be. Or definitely one of my top three. His lap, or him on top of me, or curled around me. Really, any arrangement that involved his magic hands holding me close and making me forget everything else.

I truly didn't have any expectations of Flynn. Maybe my heart was getting involved, but I would be okay. This was so healing. Just losing myself in this intense passion. Even if I thought Flynn had been embarrassed, which apparently was wrong on my part, I knew he had it bad for me when it came to sex. Things just clicked with us.

After my ex's affair with my friend, I'd been so ashamed and felt so inadequate. This thing with Flynn was so removed from my old life that I could just forget all of my baggage and grief.

Straddling his thighs, I let my hips settle over the hard ridge of his arousal. He shifted slightly, and I let out a soft gasp as pleasure zipped through me. I could feel the slick arousal between my thighs.

His eyes narrowed. "We're wearing too many clothes."

I giggled, letting my head fall into his neck and breathing in the scent of him. Flynn smelled like the wind and sometimes the ocean with a subtle woodsy hint underneath it all.

Flynn, with his tendency toward being cranky because he was always doing too much and taking care of too many people, had that unique ability to make me giggle like a girl. That carefree feeling had been in short supply for years and dwindled to nothing after Brandon died.

Lifting my head, I leaned forward and dropped a kiss on the side of his neck as I rubbed my hips over his cock. "Race you," I teased when I looked in his eyes.

Shimmying off his lap, I dashed across the living room to his bedroom. Flynn, whose stride was definitely longer than mine, caught up to me in a hot second just as I made it through the doorway. I was laughing as I tossed my T-shirt to the floor.

I didn't remember who won the race and honestly didn't care. All I knew was in maybe less than a minute, Flynn was lifting me against his naked body, every glorious inch of it, and carrying me to his bed. He stopped at the foot of it to pause and capture one of my puckered nipples with his mouth. He teased it with his tongue and a graze of his teeth. His arousal jutted between us, pressing against my belly.

"Flynn!" I gasped.

He lifted his head, and his fierce gaze met mine. "Yes, princess?"

"Hurry it up. I need you inside me."

"Well then, I'll have to take as much time as I can," he teased as he eased me down on the bed. I shimmied backward quickly, trying to take him with me. He was having none of it and curled his hands around my ankles to hold me still.

"I'm in charge tonight, princess." His voice was low and deep, causing me to shiver all over.

His palms slid up my calves, pushing my knees apart. His lips followed, like honey dripping, the kisses making glancing contact and making me desperate for more. I felt his weight press down in the mattress, and his shoulders settled between my thighs.

Flynn blew lightly on my sex, just before licking into the most intimate part of me. He was a thorough man. With slow teases of his tongue and his fingers sinking into me, I was gripping his hair as pleasure rolled through me.

I was shameless, begging and pleading, until he finally, *finally* gave me what I needed. He dragged his tongue roughly with just enough pressure over my clit and drove two fingers into me. My entire body spasmed, the climax hitting me in crashing waves.

My pleasure was still echoing in little pings through my body as he rose and settled his weight over me. His elbows framed my face, and I opened my eyes when he brushed my tangled hair away from my cheeks.

"Look at me, princess."

He brought his hips against me, and I felt the thick head of his cock nudge at my entrance.

"Flynn," I gasped when he notched a little farther in but didn't go all the way.

With his intense blue eyes on me, I felt as if all the doors to my heart were blown wide open when he slowly entered me. He held still when he was seated fully inside. My walls rippled around him from the aftershocks of my climax moments earlier. I was so sensitive. My clit was swollen, and I could feel the friction from where we were joined.

He watched me when he withdrew in increments. The slow pull and glide of his strokes in and out was intoxicating. I heard my ragged gasps and pleas. His breathing was rough, and his voice gruff. My fingers dug into his back, and I arched roughly into him.

OhDaphnebabyplease. He took in a gulp of air. *Baby, just let me...*

My next orgasm snuck up on me, striking in slow, liquid waves of pleasure as my pussy rippled and clamped around his cock, drawing his release out. He muttered something roughly, and I felt the lustrous heat of his release filling me.

Flynn fell against me, and I savored his strong weight. I only got it for a minute because he rolled us over swiftly so I was lying on top of him. I fell asleep like that with his fingers lazily sifting through my hair.

———

I hadn't realized I'd lulled myself into a sense of safety. I felt like I was finally getting my feet under me and inching past the paralyzing grief of Brandon's death. I was also, for the first time, truly accepting that the life I had before Brandon died was nothing but a shaky world that had collapsed in on itself when something *real* happened.

Raised in money and groomed to work in my family's business, the only thing I could say I really loved was my little restaurant. The only reason I got to keep that pet project, as my father had dubbed it, was because, by a stroke of luck, it made money, and it was successful. It worked for all of his investment collaborations.

Here in Alaska, with people who didn't care how much money I had, and where the moose snorting and pawing behind a tree made me feel more alive than I'd ever felt, I almost didn't recognize the person I'd been before. I couldn't believe I'd married a man who took pride in ruthlessly making money, no matter who was hurt by it.

Life returned to slap me in the face a few days after the incident with Cat. Cat and Flynn had achieved an uneasy footing after that. She told him what happened. Although I knew Flynn wanted to raise a stink with the kid, he didn't. He did, however, ground her for a week for skipping classes. That was *fun* because they were sniping at each other every day. To Flynn's credit, Cat usually started it.

I was in the pantry when I heard Cat's voice. "Excuse me, where are you going?" Cat called, sounding indignant.

"Young lady, I'm here to find my daughter."

Dread curled in my belly. I knew that voice. It was my mother. Although I hadn't really wanted to, I'd called her almost weekly since I'd been here, hoping it would keep her at bay.

I didn't even care to wonder how she found me. I was sure she'd hired a private investigator to dig into my credit cards, or Lord knows what else. I'd only told her I was going to Alaska. That was it.

My heart was hammering hard, and I felt sick. I

was suddenly cold all over and almost dropped the jar of olives in my hand. I set them carefully on the pantry shelf and turned to walk out into the kitchen.

My mother was shaking Cat's hand off her elbow. "Don't you dare touch me," she huffed.

My mother was a snob and kind of a bitch. In my own broken way, I still loved her. "Mom."

She turned, and we stared at each other for a moment. I took her in. She wore an expensive knee-length lightweight coat belted at the waist over a skirt and a pair of black leather boots with stockings. Her hair was in a tidy twist, and gold earrings dangled from her ears. The giant diamond on her wedding band flashed as she smoothed her palms on her coat.

My mind flashed to the day I met Flynn. I'd been wearing a skirt and boots on the drive here. I recalled the incredulous look on his face and realized I felt exactly the same way looking at my mother just now.

"Daphne, I'm here to get you," my mother said.

I was wearing leggings with a T-shirt and my apron loosely tied around my waist. Cat looked back and forth between us. She didn't say anything, but I sensed she was ready to have my back if necessary, and it made me want to laugh.

"I'm not going anywhere. Nice to see you, though. How was your trip, Mom?" I asked, sarcasm dripping from every word.

I felt more than saw Flynn when he came into the kitchen. After looking from my mother to me, he crossed over to stand beside me. "Can I help you?" he asked.

My mother narrowed her icy gaze at Flynn. "You can't help me with anything. I'm here to pick up my daughter."

"Oh, my God, Mom, I'm standing right here. I'm not going anywhere with you."

When my mother closed her eyes and released a breath in an annoyed huff, I realized how much I resembled her. I shared her auburn hair and green eyes and petite build. She looked strung tight and as if she was made of sharp edges.

As a mother, she was *all* sharp edges. My entire childhood had been about making sure everything looked just so, including me.

My heart was thumping erratically, and dread was an icy knot in my belly now. It wasn't that I couldn't deal with my mother. But her presence here, in a place that was mine and entirely separate from her, felt as if she were defiling it.

My mother opened her eyes again. "Daphne, please come with me," she said sternly as if I were nothing more than a little girl.

My mother counted on many things from me, and all of my life until Brandon died, I'd never hesitated to try to placate her. I did love her, no matter how well I'd come to understand her. But before brutal grief and disillusionment shredded me to pieces, I didn't do things because they felt right. I did them because the expectation had been drilled so thoroughly into me.

My son's death and my ex's affair during that terrible time had ripped the veil away from appearances. My mother was so terribly out of place here. I was too. Yet in the time I'd been here, the changes were flying fast and furious inside me.

"Mom, I'm not coming with you. I'm not sure why you took it upon yourself to fly out here, but I'm not going anywhere with you."

Flynn's palm landed in the curve at my waist, and it almost felt as if he were imparting some of his strength to me. I needed every ounce I could get. Despite our audience, I actually had to fight the urge to turn into him to seek the shelter I knew he would give. Maybe it was just sex, but that didn't matter now.

I watched my mother's eyes flick down to the small distance between Flynn and me. I knew she noticed he'd touched me and was probably already calculating what that might mean.

Her sharp eyes swept up to mine, anger and disappointment glittering in them. "I will be in Anchorage for three days. I'd like you to think about coming home."

Without another word, she spun around, the heels of her boots loud on the tile floor as she walked away. Unable to stop myself, I followed, but I kept my distance. I didn't miss the fact that Flynn was right behind me.

I watched as my mother picked her way across the gravel parking lot to climb into an all-black SUV with a driver. I couldn't fault her for that. It hadn't been the smartest plan for me to drive myself out here when I was unfamiliar with the area.

With the sound of the gravel crunching under the tires as the vehicle disappeared, I sagged against the wall in the entryway.

Flynn had been waiting a few feet away and turned to stop in front of me. "Are you okay?"

Lifting my eyes, I took a breath and nodded. "Yeah. That was my mother."

His eyes searched my face before he nodded. "I gathered. I told you I didn't like her before, and I stand behind that statement."

I gave him a rueful smile, internally surprised I wasn't all that upset. With my mother gone, my heart rate slowed, and the sick feeling in my stomach faded.

Although I would never wish it on anyone, an upside to going through a horrible loss was everything had a different perspective.

Before my son died and the accompanying mess around it, I would've thought it would've been horrible to be on bad terms with my mother and have her disappointed in me. Now, it wasn't nearly that big of a deal. Because nothing would likely measure up to the pain I felt after Brandon died. I'd walked through the barren darkness inside. I was still alive and was actually, maybe okay.

"I'm due for a flight. Wanna come with me?" Flynn asked.

As I looked up to his eyes, my heart jumped. I knew he was asking because he thought I could use a distraction. I could, and I didn't even know what to think of just how well he could read me.

"Yes, please. Where're we going?"

Chapter Twenty-Five

FLYNN

"Which street?" I asked.

"That one," Elias replied, pointing ahead.

We were in Anchorage for an unexpected trip to fetch a plane part that had arrived. We'd just picked it up and then stopped to grab lunch at what Elias claimed was the best burger place in Anchorage.

Not much later, we were enjoying our lunch when I felt a presence beside our table. Glancing up, I looked into the cool eyes of Daphne's mother. I could feel Elias's eyes on me before his gaze shifted back to Daphne's mother and then to his plate. He remained silent, taking a bite of his burger and chewing.

I repeated the same question I'd asked Daphne's mother when she appeared a few days earlier at the resort. "Can I help you?"

I figured that was really polite of me under the circumstances. Nothing I knew about Daphne's mother led me to consider her anything other than a cold bitch. In the days that passed since she'd shown up, Daphne had been unsettled and tense, kicking my protective instincts into high gear.

"I think you can," she said in that haughty voice of hers. "I'd like you to leave my daughter alone. It appears she's working for you, so I'd appreciate it if you would fire her."

Elias finished chewing and took a sip of his water. Cold anger slithered down my spine.

"No," was my only reply.

Her nostrils flared, and she narrowed her eyes at me. "You don't know who you're dealing with."

"I don't think you know who *you're* dealing with," I returned. "I don't really care either. What kind of mother would expect their daughter to work with a man who screwed around on her while her son was dying? Because that's the kind of mother you are."

Daphne's mother looked as if I slapped her hard across the face. For a split second, the façade cracked, and her pain flashed in her eyes. I didn't care if I hurt her feelings.

I wondered if this woman actually breathed. But then she took a slightly ragged breath. It was so out of character for her that I felt a twinge of guilt for being so blunt.

"Why do you care?" she finally returned.

"It doesn't matter why I care. I doubt you care all that much about how Daphne's doing. Seems to me you just care about how it looks. If you want her to come home, maybe you should try to actually give a shit."

My words were harsh, and the anger spinning inside me was so intense I wanted to punch some-thing. Not Daphne's mother. Maybe a wall would do. I just wanted her to stop and think about what Daphne had been through.

Her mother simply stared at me. For whatever reason, I think she realized she wasn't going to get what she wanted from me. She gave me a long look. "Lord knows why you want to protect my daughter. She's been nothing but a disappointment."

At that, the woman I was having a hard time considering a mother turned and left, the heels of her boots clicking on the floor.

I hadn't even realized one of my fists was balled into a tight grip until I looked over at Elias.

"You can calm down now," he said dryly.

Uncurling my fist, I laid my palm flat on the table before I reached for my water to take a sip.

"You really like Daphne," Elias offered. There was no hint of a question in his words.

"Obviously. I don't like her mother, though."

Elias chuckled. "No? I didn't notice."

At that moment, someone spoke. "Hey, guys." Glancing over, we saw Trey Holden approaching. "Shopping trip?" he asked when he stopped beside our table.

I nodded. "Parts run. You?"

"Errands and more errands. I'm actually picking up lumber because we're gonna do a small addition to the house. The new baby will make three kids, so we can use the space," he explained. "You had a chance to think about whether you want to buy my business?"

"I didn't need to think about it," I replied dryly. "I just need to follow up with the bank. I think I can make it work. Give me a few weeks?"

"Dude, you've got months. My plane's idle through the winter anyway. As long as you decide before, say, next March, we should be fine. You doing okay?" he asked.

I felt more than saw Elias's teasing grin. It said something that my brief encounter with Daphne's mother had unsettled me, so Trey might notice I was off. I shrugged. "Just dealing with some stuff."

Elias helpfully offered, "We have bets on Flynn falling in love."

"What the hell would you know about love?" I muttered as I stuffed a fry in my mouth.

A slow smile stretched across Trey's face as he glanced back and forth between Elias and me. "Is that so?"

I sighed. "Fuck my life. I don't enjoy being the subject of gossip."

Elias waggled his brows. "It's not gossip when you're sitting right here."

Trey clapped me on the shoulder. "I'll say this. Love is the best thing that ever happened to me. No need to be afraid of it."

Chapter Twenty-Six

DAPHNE

"Mom, why are you here?" We were having a video call. I'd finally called before I knew she was due to fly out.

"You're my daughter, and I would like you back home. It's important to your father and me for things to finally get back to normal. We've indulged you through this difficult year, but it's time to come home," she explained as calmly as ever.

Ever since my mother had shown up, I'd felt off-balance, and I was scrambling to get it back. I was cold all the time again and felt slightly sick. It brought up uncomfortable memories. In the first few weeks after Brandon's death, I could hardly eat. Of course, his death came after the hardest months of my life, during which I barely ate either. I'd lost more weight than was healthy.

I curled my hand around a cup of tea, needing the warmth but also needing something to hold. "Is Pete still working there?"

"Of course he is." My mother didn't even try to keep the exasperation out of her voice. "You know our two families are too intertwined for us to sever that business relationship. I am, of course, disappointed in him, but chin up and carry on."

"Oh, my God. Disappointed? You're disappointed in Pete for having an affair with one of my friends while our son was dying?"

My mother arched a brow and let out a controlled sigh. Everything she did was controlled. "You need to get over it. If it helps, Natalie was fired. They dated for about six months afterward, but they broke up after you left."

As if that would make it better. My mother was freaking incredible. "So Nat deserves to be fired, but Pete doesn't?"

"Her family has no stake in the company the way Pete's family does. It's time for you to get over these frivolous pursuits and get back to doing what you're meant to do."

I stared at my mother on the video screen on my phone and swallowed the scream in my throat.

————

That night, I lay gasping on Flynn's chest after another intense bout of sex. In my body, in my mind, in my heart, and in my soul, I felt that we were making love every time. Except I didn't think that's what Flynn considered it.

For the past few days, he'd been withdrawn, just the slightest bit more distant than before. I didn't know whether to attribute it to my mother's unexpected visit or something else. He'd gone to Anchorage for the day to do some errands. I found out by chance from Elias that they'd encountered my mother, and Flynn sort of told her off. When I'd asked him about it, he'd simply shrugged.

I didn't know what to think. Although I didn't intend to go home and return to the life I had before, I did need to return to tidy up some details.

Lifting my head, I rested my chin on my palm on his chest. As if he could feel my gaze, his eyes opened. "If I needed to take a few weeks off, would that be okay?" I asked.

I didn't know how to read his eyes as they searched my face. "Princess, you can do whatever you need. I know you don't need this job for the money. We'll make do. Are you going home?"

"Not to stay. But I do need to go deal with a few things."

A part of me wanted Flynn to ask more, but he didn't. I didn't remember falling asleep, but I did recall waking during the night as he slipped out of bed. I lay awake in the darkness, knowing he was returning to his bedroom. We had an unspoken agreement that whenever Cat was home, which she was last night, I didn't sleep there. Although she knew about us, I didn't feel right spending the night there when she was home. Because I didn't know how to define what we were.

A few days later, I searched Flynn's eyes. "I'll be back."

Flynn's touch was light as his hand brushed my hair away from my forehead. "You don't have to make promises, princess."

"I'm not leaving for good," I insisted. Because I meant it. I truly did.

He was quiet, and the space around us felt crowded with so many unspoken emotions. I had fallen in love with Flynn. I sensed he might return the feeling, but the distance that had arisen between us after my mother showed up was still here. I didn't know what to make of it.

"Call me," he said softly. "We'll miss you."

Chapter Twenty-Seven

DAPHNE

We'll miss you.

My brain couldn't let go of the "we" in that statement. Flynn hadn't been speaking of himself as an individual. It was all of them as a group who would miss me in a collective way.

Meanwhile, I missed him so acutely my heart ached from it. Oh, I missed Cat and Nora and all the guys too, yet it was only Flynn to whom my thoughts circled back to again and again.

I stood outside my family's offices in Atlanta as traffic crowded the streets. The air was warm and still humid, even in autumn. I'd always loved this city. I still did, but it was so different now. I'd spent my lifetime before Brandon died absorbing the world through the lens handed to me by my parents. Now, I knew how crisp the air could smell and the sheer glory of the wilderness outside the city. And so much more.

Even though I didn't know if Flynn loved me, it was his strength and belief in me that buoyed me when I walked into the building and prepared to face my past. I was distantly surprised at how much I wasn't falling apart.

When I entered the building lobby, I got a startled smile from the man behind the reception desk. "Hey, George," I called with a wave.

"Hello, Miss Bell. I didn't know when we would see you again." His Southern accent was like soothing honey.

I paused, wondering how long I'd known George. "How long have I known you?"

The lines on his face deepened around his eyes when he smiled. "Well, Daphne, I've been working here since you were ten years old."

His brown eyes twinkled as I reached across the desk to squeeze his hand. "Eighteen years. Wow. I missed you, although I can't say I missed the rest."

George's eyes sobered. He'd come to Brandon's funeral and also visited him in the hospital. Before Brandon was sick, George kept him company occasionally when I was racing between my restaurant and my office here.

"It's good to see you. I absolutely understand why you might not love coming back here," George said with a dip of his chin. At that moment, someone else approached the desk. With George's quick smile and the understanding in his eyes lifting me, I walked into the elevator.

During my marriage, I'd taken this elevator skyward every morning with my ex. I'd had many abrupt revelations in the months before Brandon died and the time since—death brings shocking clarity in ways nothing else can. One revelation became even more blindingly clear now.

I'd been so young when I married, fresh out of college. I didn't know better, yet I thought I knew everything. Not in an arrogant way, just in a foolish, naïve way.

At the time, I considered myself lucky to fall in love with the son of my family's closest business partners. It had almost seemed fated. Now, I knew it wasn't love. Just infatuation of a person and an idea built on the shakiest of foundations that collapsed the minute something difficult happened. It was like spun glass that shattered under the slightest pressure.

I tried to imagine Flynn in this situation with me. Although I knew he would be out of place, his tall, formidable presence would walk these hallways with more authentic confidence than my ex ever had.

As I stepped out of the elevator and saw the glass doorway into my family's business offices, I experienced a breathtaking shaft of longing for Flynn. I genuinely wasn't going to that place where I started to wonder what I really meant to him. Because it didn't matter. What we had and the nights we'd spent together were more real than anything I'd experienced before. The same was true for the friendships I'd formed in the few months I'd been in Alaska. I had survived the worst. Whether or not Flynn fell in love with me, I would be okay. But right now, I missed him dearly, and I suddenly felt weary.

I remembered how grumpy he could be and the flip side of that. I remembered the feel of his palm at the curve of my spine when my mother showed up, and the feel of him cupping my cheek when he called me princess. I lifted my chin and forced my legs forward.

Just now, I expected to feel a little sick and intimidated. The way I'd felt for months every time I tried to come to these offices while I'd been facing down my son's cancer.

Striding through the doors, I looked ahead to see Carol, the receptionist. Her eyes widened when she saw me. She recovered quickly, schooling her expression to a bland and polite one. "Good morning, Daphne."

Carol had been friends with my friend and had covered up the affair. Although Nat had been fired, I surmised no one knew about Carol's knowledge. I smiled tightly. *Okay* was the best I could describe how I was doing. "Good morning," I replied.

Brushing past her, I strolled down the hallway. I hadn't asked, but I was prepared for my office to no longer be available for me. I didn't intend to use it, but I was mildly curious. When I stopped beside the door, I saw my name was still on it, and it was locked. Sliding my key in, I stepped into the office, then closed the door behind me.

Someone must have cleaned because it was perfectly tidy. Nothing was on the surface of my desk, and the office was untouched. I hadn't come to this office since I learned of Pete's affair. That had been before Brandon even died.

I was learning I was stronger than I expected. I thought this would be painful, but it wasn't. I had already let this go. Turning, I left my office unlocked and strode down the hallway with purpose. Reaching my father's office, I knocked. When I heard him call, "Come in," I stepped inside and immediately closed the door behind me.

"Hello, Dad."

He hadn't even looked up yet. I did have one thing on my side: surprise. His eyes whipped up. "Daphne! I didn't know you were here."

"I know. I'm sure George or Carol tried to buzz you."

My father glanced at his phone and cast a wry smile.

He rose from his chair and rounded his desk. I stood in front of it, my fingertips resting on the edge of the desk. When he stopped in front of me, I was surprised to see regret and sadness pass through his eyes. "I just want you to know I'm sorry," he said slowly, his voice gruff.

This shocked me. I didn't realize my mouth dropped open for a moment. As soon as I did, I snapped it shut. "For what?"

"For not putting you first." My father pulled me into a hug, his arms folding around me.

After a moment where I was frozen, I returned the hug before stepping back. "I'm not coming back to work here. I came to tell you that in person."

My father strode to stare out the windows, which looked out over downtown Atlanta. After a moment, he returned to his desk and rested his hips against it. "I understand. I actually looked into whether we could unwind the partnership with Pete's family. It's a remote possibility, but nothing that can happen quickly from a legal perspective. I was going to ask what you would like me to do."

Of all the things I had anticipated and steeled myself to face, this wasn't one of them. Giving myself a mental shake, I shrugged. "Even if you go through the trouble to do that, I'm not going to work here. It brings me no joy. Do what's best for the business."

My father's eyes searched my face, his gaze shrewd and assessing. After a moment, he nodded. "Understood. Well then, I'm only going to make one change."

"What's that?"

"I'm only going to keep the partnership intact if Pete is no longer working here. Because it's been a hard year and it's been messy, I've left it alone. But that'll be the one change I'll make."

My surprise must've shown on my face again. My father regarded me quietly before striding to look out the windows again. The set of his shoulders was stiff, and he exuded a sense of weariness.

"There are many things I haven't gotten right in this lifetime, Daphne. But asking you to consider staying on after what happened with Pete will remain one of my biggest regrets."

I waited quietly. I couldn't say I was happy about this. It was more that, for the first time in my life, I felt as if my father was trying to understand.

Turning back to look at me, he continued, "I'm sorry. Your mother is still struggling because she wants you to come home. I told her that perhaps she needs to make the choice of whether to have a relationship with you at all."

I swallowed through the emotion lodging in my throat and nodded slowly. "It's not my personality to never talk to you or her, but this year has brought some things into focus. You didn't have to, but thank you for making the decision about Pete. Honestly, I'm not going to be working here, so if it's better for the business to keep him, that's fine."

My father shook his head slightly. "It's not really a business decision. Well, I suppose it is. Our family controls fifty-one percent of this company, and his family controls forty-nine percent. It's taken me a while to come to this, but I can't work effectively with someone who would do what he did to you. So, there you go. Does your mother know you're here?"

"I was just going to see her next. I didn't call ahead."

My father chuckled softly. "Well, I know that, dear.

My phone would've been blowing up from her if you had."

I stepped to him, and he hugged me firmly before drawing back and squeezing my shoulders. As his hands fell away, he asked, "What is your plan?"

"I don't know."

I left my father's office and walked up the stairs to the top floor where my mother's office was. Over the years, my mother had held different positions in the company. Within the last decade, she almost exclusively handled the charitable projects for the business, a small but very busy operation.

My father's question echoed in my thoughts. *What is your plan?*

I honestly didn't know. I had some ideas, but no more than that. I would wing it, and it would be okay. I was starting to understand I would live with a jagged scar in my heart from losing my son for the rest of my life. But scar tissue is stronger than the original tissue after it heals.

I remembered Flynn's eyes, that glacial blue with the charcoal rim. I heard him say "princess" in my thoughts again and again. I felt my lips curling in a smile at recalling how much he'd initially annoyed me and just what a grumpy guy he could be.

Another shaft of longing pierced me. I missed him. I knew I would get over him. I would go back to Alaska, and I would cook there. Then I would probably leave when it felt right because I didn't know if Flynn could ever let down his guard enough to love anyone, and I never wanted him to change.

When I knocked on my mother's door, it whipped open. She stood there, practically vibrating with energy. "Your father just called to let me know you were here. Why didn't you call and let us know you were coming home?" She all but yanked me into her office. "Thank goodness you had enough sense to—" She stopped talking when I looked at her sharply.

"Mom, let's not talk about how much sense you think I have about anything. I came back to officially let you know I'm not returning to work here."

"You'll re-open your restaurant then." She said this firmly, as if it were a task already executed. As if re-opening my small café was quick and easy.

I shook my head again. "I don't think so. I'm going to figure out what I want to do. While I do that, I have a job in Alaska, and I don't intend to leave them hanging."

My mother sighed, pursing her lips. "Have you fallen for that man?"

I wasn't about to go into my feelings for Flynn with my mother. "Mom, it doesn't matter. I'm not working here, and I don't plan to live in Atlanta. I'll come to visit, and we'll be fine. As for what I'm doing and who I'm in love with, it doesn't really matter."

My mother's lips pressed into a thin line, and I was shocked to see the sheen of tears in her eyes. "I don't like having you so far away," she finally said.

"Mom, I don't know where I'll end up, but it won't be here. That's just not what I want. Maybe that will change, but for now, I know that. Can you just try to understand?"

My mother's eyes, so similar to my own, lifted. She regarded me quietly. "I'm trying. Did your father tell you he's making it a condition of the partnership that Pete leaves his position?"

I nodded. "That still doesn't change my mind, and I told him that."

My mother let out a soft breath and gave a sharp nod. "How long will you be here?"

"A few days."

My mother, who'd never been the warmest person even when times were good, stepped to me and lifted her hands to squeeze my shoulders. "I love you, Daphne. I don't understand, but I will try."

She leaned forward and pressed a kiss to my cheek, the height of affection for my mother. "Where are you staying?" she asked when she stepped back.

"Well, I hoped with you and Dad."

"Of course. We'll have dinner together tonight."

Chapter Twenty-Eight

DAPHNE

I saved my visit to Brandon's grave until the morning before my flight to leave. Maybe it wasn't the best plan, but I didn't want to dally in Atlanta after that. As it was, everywhere I went, it felt as if memories were hitting me like rocks in an avalanche. I was dodging them constantly so I didn't get emotionally flattened.

As I was loading my suitcase into my rental car, my phone vibrated. Although I had deleted Pete's number from my phone, I still knew it by heart. I felt the vibration in my palm as I stared at the screen and then decided I might as well get this over with. Avoidance wasn't something that helped.

Sliding my thumb across the screen, I lifted the phone to my ear. "Hello?"

"Daphne, it's Pete. I heard you were in the office the other day."

"I was."

That was three days ago, and he was just now calling. I waited to see what prompted his call.

"I need you to talk to your father."

I almost started laughing hysterically. When the

veil had been lifted from my eyes about just how shallow the affection in my marriage had been, Pete had stopped trying to put on a show. I knew he deeply loved our son, but I had no illusions that he ever loved me. I think he saw our marriage as a beneficial business alliance.

"About what?"

"Apparently, he's making my departure from my position in the company conditional on not dividing the company. Did you put him up to this?"

"Absolutely not. I don't intend to return to my position there. My father made that decision on his own and was simply waiting to talk to me about it. I'll leave it to you to figure out how to handle it. Is that all you wanted to discuss?"

I was kind of shocked at how calm I was. I suppose it was because I had truly moved on from Pete and the illusion of what I thought we had.

Pete was quiet. I sensed he didn't know how to deal with me like this. When I found out about his affair, I was crushed and hysterical. I shifted from that to cold anger, and then my entire focus shifted to dealing with Brandon being sick and dying. Through all of that, Pete assumed a somewhat polite stance. When I filed for divorce, he'd put up a small fight and then backed down quickly when I hired a well-known ruthless attorney.

Apparently, his attorney had enough sense to know how bad it looked in court for him. After several quiet beats, Pete spoke. "I know it's been a shitty year. For what it's worth, I'm really sorry. I miss Brandon."

Grief struck me so hard that I lost my breath. Although I didn't miss Pete and now had a clear-eyed view of what our relationship had never actually been, we'd shared a terrible loss. I knew no one else could understand my pain the way he did.

When I could catch my breath, I said, "I know you do. You were the best father to him. Even though I obviously don't like how you treated me, that doesn't change the fact that I know how much you loved him."

Pete was really quiet, to the point I thought maybe he wasn't on the phone anymore. When he spoke again, I could hear the tears in his voice. "You're absolutely right. I was a shitty husband, but I loved Brandon, and I'll never stop missing him."

We sat in silence on that phone line, and a strange sense of peace gusted through me. "You can call me if you ever need to," I finally said. "I do wish you the best, Pete."

I didn't remember how we said goodbye, but we hung up. That was one of the paradoxes I had learned. Everybody had different facets to who they were— some good, some neutral, some clumsy, some bad. Pete was shallow and superficial in many ways, yet he was also a good father to Brandon. He'd never been a hands-off kind of dad. He changed diapers, he fed him bottles during the night, and he never hesitated to take him to do things.

I could appreciate and honestly love that about him and for the gift it gave to our son. I could also see him for the man he was as a husband, which was hurtful to me and nothing I wanted to repeat.

I gathered my strength back together, almost like wrapping a coat around my shoulders, and finished packing my suitcase. A short drive later, I walked to the small plaque. *Brandon Lind. 2014 - 2018. He was light, love, laughter, and joy. May his memory live for eternity.*

For mostly the first month after Brandon died, I

almost couldn't cry. I felt tied tight like a knot, the kind where you try to pick it out with your fingers and you can never get purchase to loosen it. When I finally loosened the knot, the tears came in noisy bursts, and it almost hurt to even talk to anyone. It was as if my skin itself was carrying the wounds of my grief, sensitive to air, to light, and to the mere presence of anyone who knew what had happened.

During those months, it was easier to be around strangers because they didn't know. I could pretend I was okay. Strangely, it wasn't denial. It was more like practice for keeping my shit together. Because I couldn't do it around anyone who knew what happened. Just their knowledge was enough of a reminder that I would fall apart.

Then came the next stage—the anger. I swung between anger and denial and a sort of crazy wishful thinking. Even now, I still knew exactly where I had one outfit for Brandon should he mysteriously reappear. I even brought that outfit in my luggage to Alaska. It was during the height of my anger that I finally saw a therapist.

Among many things, she'd assured me I wasn't absolutely insane to keep an outfit of Brandon's. Apparently, that was a thing people did. It was a type of magical thinking when someone died. When death was unexpected, she told me people had all kinds of weird thoughts, and that hope—no matter how wildly irrational at times—helped to carry us through the pain.

I learned that the winding path of grief had no logical order. It was different for everyone, and my process was exactly the way it needed to be for me. It was odd to consider it now, but I realized in hindsight that my anger toward Pete and Nat had actually given me some strength during the worst times.

I knelt in the grass and traced my fingers over his name. I fingered the locket that held one of his auburn curls. Aside from the random advertisement that popped up on my screen when I saw the name of Flynn's resort, I'd started looking for travel in Alaska because Brandon always wanted to go. I didn't even remember what started that wish for him. I thought it was perhaps an episode from one of the nature shows he loved to watch. We limited his screen time, but he often selected those shows when he got his half hour. He got sick so fast. We didn't even have time to take a trip.

So I made that trip for him and for me. Now, I didn't know if I would stay there or go somewhere else. Maybe I would come back here someday. I just didn't know.

"I love you, bear," I whispered. We ended up calling him Brandon-bear, which shortened to bear when he was still a baby. The nickname stuck.

I lingered for a few minutes before standing. As I drove to the airport, Flynn circled through my thoughts. He was always there, always feathering along the edges. Although I still felt uncertain about where my life might take me, I would go back and see what happened next.

Pulling my phone out, I used voice to text to send a message to Flynn. *I'll be landing in Anchorage tomorrow.*

I wanted to say more, but it didn't feel right.

Chapter Twenty-Nine

FLYNN

"Flynn, I'm not a little girl. You're being an ass," Cat said, her cheeks red and her eyes practically spitting fire as she glared at me.

"Cat, this is the second time you've skipped afternoon classes. Daphne isn't here to pick you up, so you've got me. I thought you decided this guy was a jerk."

Cat suddenly burst into tears and turned away in her seat to stare out the window. She wrapped her arms tightly around her waist. God help me. I didn't handle tears well.

Nora was the first one Cat had texted with her dilemma, but she was at a doctor's appointment this afternoon and wasn't available. Nora had texted me right before I was supposed to take off for a tourist flight. Tucker had graciously taken over for me, and I'd zoomed over to pick Cat up at the address Nora texted me.

Not knowing what to say to Cat and figuring anything I said was a bad option, I put my truck in gear and started driving home. After a few minutes, I said, "Look, I get that maybe you like him, and maybe you want to impress him. I'm guessing he pressured you again. You don't have to tell me if I'm right, and personally, I'd prefer to be wrong. Maybe he's not a total ass, but I'm guessing he wants to get laid because that's what most guys wanna do when they're his age and frankly, into their twenties and even later."

I heard Cat laugh a little bit, so I kept going. "You're not allowed to hang out with him at all anymore. I'm sure you have feelings about that, but it is what it is. You already know you're not supposed to skip class. You're grounded for a week, and I'll talk to the principal about what the school plans to do."

I drove along in silence, wishing Daphne were here. I knew from her text this morning she would be here tomorrow, but that didn't seem soon enough.

Cat wouldn't even look in my direction. Every time I glanced toward her in the passenger seat, her head was turned to look out the window. She sniffled a few times, and my heart cracked with every sniffle. I hated, absolutely hated, seeing Cat hurt.

She'd always been such a spirited girl. She wasn't really a tomboy. Although in Alaska, she was typical. She knew how to manage a rifle, she'd helped me and Grant deal with a moose carcass once, she knew how to change the oil in my truck, and she was shaping up to be a great mechanic for our small planes. She knew her way around the woods and was savvy in the outdoors. She was all of that, and she was also very feminine. She liked to look good when it came to any kind of social activity.

I wanted to kick this guy's ass, but I knew Cat would be beyond embarrassed if I intervened. All I could do was tell her he was being a jerk and forbade her from going to his place again. Then I'd pray she wouldn't. She might anyway. Depending on what else I learned, I might talk with his parents.

Daphne had been with us for over two months before she left for Atlanta, and winter was nipping at the heels of autumn already. In that short time, it hadn't escaped my notice that Cat opened up more easily with Daphne than the rest of us. Probably because like most teenagers, Daphne seemed more neutral and didn't have the emotionally loaded connections of siblings. She was also the closest thing to a mother Cat had after our mom died. Nora and Cat were too close in age.

Of course, the unwelcome distraction of Cat skipping school was barely enough to knock my brain off the loop of Daphne it had been playing.

I wondered how she was doing. I didn't even like to think about how much I missed her. I *missed* her.

After we got back, Cat sequestered herself in her bedroom. I found Diego in the kitchen, rummaging in the large pantry. "Are you cooking tonight?" he asked when he straightened and saw me walking in.

"Yup. Daphne flies in tomorrow."

"Thank God," Diego muttered.

He opened the refrigerator and snagged a beer. Looking my way, he held one aloft, his question unspoken.

"Yes, please." I caught the beer he tossed between us in one hand and reached for the bottle opener in the drawer right by my hip.

"So Daphne's actually coming back?" Diego mused before opening his beer and taking a long swallow.

I nodded and walked into the pantry to figure out what the hell I was going to make for our guests tonight. "How does salmon fillets with rice and vegetables sound for dinner?" I asked as I returned to the kitchen with the rice already in hand.

"Serviceable," he replied.

I rolled my eyes and snagged a package from the freezer with enough flash-frozen fillets for the group who was here this evening. When I started cooking, Diego helped. He was actually a solid cook himself, but I didn't pay him to do that. I always appreciated it when he helped, though, because he had a better instinct for seasonings than I did.

We worked quietly for a bit. Diego finished measuring the rice, and then commented, "Heard from Trey that you're set to buy him out next spring. That all settled?"

"Oh, yeah. Sorted out a loan with the bank. We could use another plane and his customers. We also get him for backup whenever he's got time," I replied.

"Smart move." Diego stepped to the sink to rinse his hands. I was adjusting the flame under the rice when he added, "Speaking of smart, you get smart yet about Daphne?"

I ended up turning the flame up instead of down. Diego snorted and gestured with his elbow toward it as he dried his hands. "Fuck," I muttered. After adjusting it properly, I looked toward him. "What do you mean?"

"I think you thought she wasn't coming back."

He was spot-on, and I hated to admit it. I'd thought she would leave and discover the life she had before coming here was the life she preferred. For a second, I was tempted to dismiss him, but like every guy who followed me here from my unit in the Air Force, I trusted Diego deeply and completely. He might give me shit and tease me, but he always had my best interests at heart.

"You're right."

"Sooooo?"

"I don't know, man. We're from two different worlds."

"So are we, but you're still like a brother to me. Dude, you grew up here. It's cold and beautiful. I grew up in a baked landscape of Texas. I've fallen in love with the land here, and you're like family to me. Don't give me that bullshit about coming from different worlds. Lots of people come from different worlds, but in the end, it doesn't matter." He curled his fist and thumped it over his chest quickly. "That's what matters."

My heart gave a rib-cracking kick as if it had actually heard Diego. I took a deep breath and paused to finish my bottle of beer. Tossing it in the recycle bin, I stirred the rice before replying, "I don't know what the hell I'm doing."

"Well, yeah, that's obvious," he teased. I rolled my eyes, and his gaze sobered. "I've never seen you the way you are about her. Be smart."

"Dude, I have zero healthy relationship examples. My mom was awesome and had terrible judgment in men. I never met my father, and my stepfather was an asshole who used her and was barely emotionally available for his kids."

Diego gave me a speculative look, his tongue pressing in his cheek, something he did whenever he was thinking. "I haven't been in love, but before my parents died, they were madly in love ever since I could remember. They were passionate about love and about fighting," he offered with a chuckle. "They'd have done anything for each other. I wasn't sure how you felt about Daphne until you didn't tell her how you felt before she left."

Confused, I cocked my head to the side. "Huh?"

"Maybe you didn't think this consciously, but I think you chose not to tell her how much she meant to you because you were worried it would affect whether she went home and whether she decided to come back. You didn't put your finger on the scale because you care enough that you want it to be her choice."

"Whoa, that's deep," Elias said as he walked into the kitchen, hearing the end of Diego's comments.

I cast him a glare, and he winked. He got his own beer out of the refrigerator before looking back and forth between us. "What would we do without Diego here to advise us on life and love?" he teased affectionately.

Diego rolled his eyes. "Flynn's stupid."

Elias cast me a penetrating look as his smile faded. "He's right, you know?"

———

Daphne was persistent at staying in my thoughts for the rest of the evening and into the night. Although she was always persistent. I had no willpower when it came to Daphne.

That night as I lay in bed alone, my hand curled over my arousal for a moment. Perversely, I didn't give in to the urge to satisfy myself. I needed Daphne.

I also needed a dose of nerves. Here I thought I had nerves of steel because of my years in the military, yet a woman who maybe cleared five feet and was small enough for me to carry ten miles, intimidated the hell out of me.

Chapter Thirty

FLYNN

I waited just outside the security area at the airport. I'd replied to Daphne's text to ask what time she would land, but all she'd said was she was renting a car. I'd been surprised to get an email to our business email from Daphne's mother this morning. With Daphne's travel itinerary, of all things. Her mother had also very politely asked if someone could pick Daphne up at the airport because she didn't think Daphne would ask herself. Her mother was worried about her taking a long drive on her own even though she knew she'd already done it before.

People started to file through the doors, cueing me that the flight landed. I waited impatiently to see Daphne's auburn hair. Although she was short, I was tall enough to see over most of the crowd, and I didn't miss the moment she came into my line of sight.

My pulse started rioting, and that familiar electricity sizzled through my body. When she came through the glass doors, I stepped away from the wall. Her gaze was aimed down at the floor, so I took a moment to absorb her.

She was wearing a blouse with a skirt and boots again, and my heart nearly kicked its way out of my chest. I forgot how damn cute she was in a skirt.

"Daphne."

Her head whipped up. She looked the other way first, and it took several seconds for her gaze to land on me. But when she saw me, her eyes widened, and she crossed to me immediately. "Flynn," she began, her tone wondering. "I didn't know you were coming to get me. I was going to rent a car."

With emotion rushing through me, I found I couldn't speak, so I just stepped closer and pulled her into my arms. She relaxed against me immediately, winding her arms around my waist and tucking her head into my shoulder.

Resting my cheek against her hair, I simply breathed her in—the feel of her, the scent of her, just her. Her mere presence steadied me and helped me get my internal bearings again. She lifted her head, her eyes searching mine.

"Your mom emailed and asked someone to come get you. I wanted to anyway, but you were kinda vague about your landing time."

I couldn't hold back my chuckle when Daphne's eyes widened comically. "My mother emailed you? Are you serious?"

"Oh yeah. I'm glad because that was way better than showing up here and waiting all day. I didn't know your connecting flight, so I wasn't sure where you were coming from."

Her nose wrinkled, and she cast a sheepish smile. "I didn't want to impose."

"I love it when you impose," I said in a teasing tone, but I was dead serious.

She bit her lip, her smile unfurling slowly. "It's good to see you."

Someone bumped into her from behind. "Do you have luggage?" I asked, tucking her to my side as I turned.

"Just one bag."

"Let's go get it." I couldn't stop touching her, so I curled my hand around hers as we walked.

"How was your trip?" I asked when we paused to wait near the baggage claim.

She looked up at me with those gorgeous green eyes, her gaze thoughtful. "It was what I needed. It's good to be back."

"It's good to have you back."

————

With winter approaching, the days were getting shorter. We watched the sun make its glorious bow as we drove south along Turnagain Arm, where the road hugged the feet of the mountains on one side with the waters of Cook Inlet immediately to the other side of the road. The view was stark and stunning.

"Oh, wow," Daphne breathed as she looked ahead to the snow-covered mountain peaks stained by the setting sun in a translucent pink and lavender.

"That's alpenglow." I felt Daphne look my way and glanced sideways briefly, getting a little jolt just from meeting her eyes before I brought mine back to the road. "It's the reflection from the sun."

"It looks like termination dust has fallen," she commented.

"Princess, you sound like an Alaskan now talking about termination dust," I teased.

Because I couldn't resist, I peeked her way again,

quickly bringing my eyes back to the winding highway in front of me. That brief look was enough to see her cheeks stained pink.

"Cat told me about it."

I chuckled. "Good. You know, you've come a long way since the day I found you waving in the middle of the road."

I felt rather than saw Daphne's smile. "I've never been one to back down from learning something new. I like it here. However, I don't see myself flying a plane or fighting off bears."

I laughed. "I might fly planes almost every day, but I'm not stupid enough to try to fight off a bear."

"How is Cat?" Daphne asked next.

Taking a deep breath, I didn't even try to hide my sigh. "I had to pick her up yesterday at that kid's house. I grounded her for a week again, and she's not allowed to go anywhere with him. She was crying, and it was awful. In fact, she locked herself in her room last night and hasn't spoken to me since. She came out to go to school, so I actually saw her, but she refused to speak."

"Oh, Cat," Daphne said, the empathy clear in her voice. "Being a teenager is miserable, especially a teenage girl."

"Can you please tell me why she would skip classes with him again? After what happened the last time, I don't really get it. I did tell her that guys are kind of jerks, and they're horny. I didn't say it like that, though," I added hurriedly.

Daphne's giggle made me want to stop driving and kiss her, but I didn't. Darkness was falling as I continued driving.

"I'm not Cat, so I don't really know. Most teenage girls have poor self-esteem. There's even research on this. Obviously, she liked this guy before, so he probably convinced her he wasn't going to pressure her."

"But Cat is so bossy and strong and..." I shook my head. "I don't understand."

Daphne reached over and squeezed my knee. The moment her hand moved away, I wanted it back. "It's not that simple. Cat can be bossy and strong and confident in some areas and still not feel great about herself in other areas. We don't live in a world that's kind to girls. It's particularly brutal when you're a teenager."

"Soooo," I began slowly, "it's probably a bad idea if I show up at this guy's house and give him hell?"

"Absolutely. Unless he pushed her too far after she told him no. If that's the case, you're still going to be reasonable and talk to his parents. Even if he is an asshole, he's only sixteen too. Did she tell you what happened?"

"Did you miss the part when I told you she didn't talk to me last night and this morning?" I asked dryly.

This time, Daphne's laugh was soft and understanding. "Got it. Do you think she's talked to Nora about it?"

"Nora said she didn't. I was kind of hoping Cat would talk to you."

"Me?" Daphne's voice squeaked, and she sounded startled.

"Yes, you. It's that thing. I might not have experience being a teenage girl, but I have experience being a teenager. I do remember that sometimes it's easier to talk to people where there's not as much—" I stopped talking abruptly because I didn't know how to describe what I meant.

"Emotional crap?" Daphne offered helpfully.

"Yes, that. She trusts you. Do you mind trying to talk to her?"

"Of course not, but not tonight. By the time I get there, it'll be late, so I'll try tomorrow. Maybe I can pick her up after school and take her for coffee or something."

"Whatever you think will work." I was so relieved Daphne was willing to try to talk with Cat, I honestly didn't care what she did.

"Car rides are great because she can talk without having to deal with eye contact."

I chuckled. "True." I paused before prompting, "So tell me about your trip."

Deafening quiet fell for a moment, and my heart started thumping erratically. I had enough sense to know her going home was filled with emotional land-mines. As open and honest as Daphne was about what had happened, I didn't know what she wanted to share with me. It was big, *really* big, for me to be trying to traverse this emotional territory.

I almost sagged with relief when she spoke. "It was hard, but it was good. Since I know you haven't seen the best of my mother, you might be surprised to learn we're sort of at peace right now."

"Good to know," I said gruffly, and I meant it. Even though I thought Daphne's mother had been harsh, I'd been through enough in life to know people were messy and complicated. You could do shitty things and still love a person.

My hand found its way to Daphne's as I drove through the darkness. The silence between us felt comfortable. As the miles passed, the air around us began to feel charged. Emotions were bouncing around inside my chest, and there was so much I wanted to say. There was one small problem: words had never been my strong suit. I was definitely an action kind of guy.

The depth of how much I missed Daphne twined like a vine within my unexpected feelings for her. That vine tangled even more strongly around the powerful and unrelenting need I felt for her. I wasn't even thinking when I hastily turned off the highway to an overlook through a small copse of trees.

"Where—?" Daphne's question cut off abruptly when I stopped the truck and put it in park.

For the first time ever, I was annoyed at the presence of the console between the two front seats in my truck. Given my height, my seat was already as far back as it could go. The moment Daphne's eyes caught mine, I saw the answering flare of desire in hers. It felt as if we created our own electricity, so blazing hot that it heated the space around us.

Leaning over the console, I slid my hand roughly in her hair and claimed her mouth in a fierce kiss. I growled in my throat. Daphne didn't hesitate to open her mouth and glide her tongue against mine. There was nothing graceful or controlled about the next few minutes as I pulled her over onto my lap.

Her head bumped against the roof, and I murmured, "Sorry," against her throat when her elbow hit the driver's side window.

"You should wear skirts more often," I gasped as my head fell against the seat, and I slid my palms up her thighs. Goose bumps pebbled over the surface of her skin. "Baby, you're cold."

"It wasn't cold when I got on the plane." Her words ended on a little moan as I reached her panties and dragged a knuckle over the damp silk.

She gasped again when I push the silk out of the way to find her hot and slick with arousal.

"Flynn," she murmured into my throat when her forehead fell to my neck and her hips rocked into my touch.

"Yeah, princess?"

She reached between us and boldly dragged her palm over the hard ridge of my arousal. My cock was so swollen that I could feel the tines of my zipper pressing against it.

Then I was groaning when she unzipped me quickly and shoved my jeans just far enough out of the way that my cock bounced free. "Daphne," I groaned, my voice a guttural, rough sound.

We fumbled, and then my cockhead was pressing at her entrance, and I slid home in one stroke.

I might not have the words, but I knew how to love Daphne with my hands, with my mouth, with my lips, my tongue, my teeth, and all of me. The moment I was buried to the hilt inside her and felt the ripple of her around me, I pressed an open-mouthed kiss against her neck. I tugged roughly at her blouse, snapping a few buttons. I savored every little sound she made.

Chapter Thirty-One

DAPHNE

Flynn filled me, and the slick fusion where we were joined created friction that already had me teetering on the edge of release. He nudged into me with subtle rolls, controlling the motion of my hips as I rose up and sank down.

My pulse was galloping, and I felt drunk with pleasure. My unexpected, emotional reaction to seeing him in the airport was rushing through me and tangling up with sensation. I felt as if I were going to burst into flames from the intensity of it all.

Like always, Flynn knew exactly what I needed. Right as I began to feel desperate, chasing for the release that was just out of my grasp, his hand slid down my back and gripped my hip tightly. I could feel his fingers pressing into my flesh when he muttered, "Come on, princess. Give it to me."

He pressed a hot kiss on the sensitive skin behind my ear. He adjusted our angle, and the slippery friction over my clit sent me flying apart as I cried out. My climax crashed through me roughly. I heard myself gasping his name and felt the heat of his release filling me. He growled my name against my throat.

We stayed like that for several long moments. Our cheeks were pressed together where I'd buried my face against his neck. I was almost in a stupor and boneless from the force of our coupling. I felt the soft press of his lips on the side of my neck before he lifted his head and rested it against the seat.

It took an effort to lift my head. When I met his now-familiar gaze, my heart started racing, and my entire body shuddered from the emotion that slammed into me like an earthquake.

"I missed you," Flynn said, surprising me with his words and the gravity in his tone. "In case that wasn't obvious." His lips kicked up at the corner with a wry smile.

I wanted to tell Flynn I'd fallen in love with him, but somehow this didn't seem like the right moment for that. I lifted a hand and smoothed his mussed hair. "I missed you too. In case that wasn't obvious."

His smile stretched to the other corner of his mouth when I repeated his words.

"Do we need to worry about anybody driving up?" I asked as I only now took stock of where we were. I looked out into the darkness to see the moon rising over the mountains in the distance.

"If it was summer, yes. But then if it was summer, it would be daylight, and there would be a lot more tourists. I suppose we should go."

I couldn't bring myself to move yet. Flynn looked at me and traced his thumb over my lips before leaning forward for a quick, hard kiss.

"I'm contemplating whether it's safe to drive with you in my lap," he added when he leaned back.

"It's definitely not." I laughed and felt my channel convulse slightly around him with it.

I reluctantly disentangled myself from him and crawled back into my seat with a little assist from him. After we put our clothes back to rights, Flynn leaned over and gave me a lingering kiss, sending my heart into overdrive.

Chapter Thirty-Two

DAPHNE

"No, I'm done with him," Cat said with a little huff. She reached up and tightened her ponytail. "What next?"

It was six in the morning, and Cat had shown up in the kitchen an hour earlier, announcing she wanted to learn to cook better. I'd been back for four days now and hadn't yet had an opportunity to actually talk to Cat as Flynn had hoped. He understood it wasn't something I could force, but he'd also asked me about it every night. It made my heart squeeze a little every time because he loved his little sister, and he was worried. He wore his confidence and typical grumpiness with such ease that it was almost endearing to witness his uncertainty about how to handle his teenage sister.

Flynn and I had settled into the routine we had before, late nights together, usually in my room. Although we weren't hiding that there was something between us, I still wasn't comfortable spending the night in the private quarters he shared with Cat here at the resort.

I'd largely come to terms with my feelings for him, but I could feel the sliver of distance Flynn kept between us. Except when we were naked. Then everything was vulnerable and bare. If our bodies could talk, we'd be all set.

The sex was still incredible, but it didn't seem a good message to send to Cat that we were having wild sex without any commitment, especially at her age. I didn't think Flynn was ready to acknowledge the feelings between us, and I was remarkably at peace with that. For now.

I gestured toward two onions I'd set on the counter earlier. "We need to chop those for the scrambled eggs."

"Onions in the eggs?"

"Yes. Onions make everything better, Cat. You probably haven't even noticed the sautéed onions in other things I've made. The knife on the cutting board I already set out is the best one. Cut the ends of the onion off, and then slice them in half. Then you can peel off the skin and start chopping."

Cat followed my instructions precisely and didn't ask anything further as she began chopping them. Meanwhile, I put a large sauté pan on the stove and drizzled olive oil in it before turning the burner on low. "Give it a sec, and then you can start putting the onions in the pan."

Cat kept chopping as she looked up briefly and nodded.

I decided to take my chances. "I'm sure you can guess Flynn is wondering why you might've gone back to Jonathon's house."

Cat kept her eyes down when she answered, "Well, duh. Of course, I knew that."

"I did say I thought you would guess that," I countered.

Cat snorted a laugh when she placed the knife down. I lifted the pan to swirl it and make sure the olive oil was coating the entire surface before setting it back down. "Go ahead and add the onions." I gestured to the pan.

"I don't know why I went," Cat began as she carefully scraped the onions from the cutting board into the pan. "Jonathon said he was sorry, and it wasn't like I didn't enjoy kissing him. I just didn't want things to go further. Since he apologized, I thought he understood."

"And he didn't?" I prompted.

I was discovering cooking was just as convenient as driving for potentially difficult conversations. We were both occupied doing tasks that didn't require too much concentration, so we could chat without looking directly at each other. I didn't mind the eye contact, but I knew Cat would squirm under too much focused attention.

Cat let out a sigh as she turned to rinse the cutting board. "Flynn kind of said boys are dumb and just want to have sex."

I laughed. "They kind of are, especially at that age. If Jonathon won't respect your boundaries twice, then he's shown you he won't respect your boundaries. It's that simple."

Cat's sigh was hefty this time. "Right. He told me I'm a prude. It's so stupid."

Now came the hard part. Without me asking, Cat had already started to stir the onions. "Have you heard that he said anything? I know rumors are like a brushfire in high school."

"Not yet. Even though he's a jerk, he knows I have plenty of friends."

"You do. Because you're a good friend," I said firmly. "Do you mind if I ask another question?"

"Uh, no," she replied uncertainly.

I forged ahead. She hadn't shut me out yet. "Did he push too hard? Is it something Flynn should talk to his parents, or the school, or even someone else about?"

Cat was really quiet, and I stole a quick look at her to see that she didn't look overly upset. After a moment, she looked over at me. "That's kind of heavy."

"It is. This is a serious question, and it's important."

Cat looked back at the onions and stirred them idly. "No, he didn't do anything where Flynn should talk to his parents, or the school, or the police. I guess that's who you mean by someone else." She set the spatula down so she could add air quotes to "someone else." "He just pressured me really hard. I told him to fuck off. I cried because I felt like an idiot for believing him again. I didn't cry in front of him this time. I waited in the driveway for Flynn to pick me up. Let me tell you, I wish you hadn't been out of town," she offered emphatically.

I was grating cheese. I set the grater down before turning and pulling Cat into a quick hug. "You're just fine. I'm actually glad it was Flynn instead of me."

When I stepped back and slid my palms down her arms, I was surprised to see the tiniest hint of a sheen of tears in her eyes. She wrinkled her nose and turned to check on the onions again. "Why would you say that? He grounded me," she muttered.

"Didn't he ground you for a few days the first time?"

"Well, yeah, but…"

"But what? You need to be crystal clear that I will not keep things like this from Flynn. Ever."

Cat cast me a faux glare and then burst out laughing. "I can always hope."

At that moment, the door from their apartment swung open, and Flynn came striding into the kitchen. He glanced at us as he made a beeline for the coffee pot. "What are you doing up so early, Cat?"

"Daphne's teaching me how to cook better."

Flynn's gaze caught mine for a moment, lingering just long enough to send a flush of heat racing over my skin. He tore his eyes from mine, turning to focus on his task as he poured coffee in a mug. "Seeing as she's the best cook I've ever met, you're in good hands."

Turning, he sipped his coffee and paused beside Cat to tweak the end of her ponytail. "You have a half hour before I need to take you up to meet the bus."

"I know," she replied quickly.

At that moment, Elias passed through to snag his own cup of coffee. While he and Flynn briefly conferred about the day's flight schedule, I encouraged Cat to go take her shower. I'd learned she had a tendency to wait until the absolute last moment to get ready for school.

Between her racing off to get ready for school and Elias moving on out, Flynn and I were alone in the kitchen for a few minutes. He set his coffee mug on the counter. Stepping behind me, he pressed hot kisses on the side of my neck, and it felt like drops of warm honey on my skin.

"How come you won't sleep with me every night?" he murmured. "What do I have to do to convince you?"

I turned in his arms, resting my hips against the

counter as I looked up at him. "You don't have to do anything to convince me. I just don't think it's a great idea for Cat."

"She knows we're together," he replied.

I lifted a hand and smoothed an errant lock of his hair. "I know she does, but we're not quite on the same page, and I don't want to make things complicated."

Flynn looked confused, so I simply decided to tell the truth. That always tended to clear the air. "I have no expectations, but I love you. I'm pretty sure that's not where things are for you."

Flynn looked shell-shocked. He stared at me and opened his mouth to speak before giving his head a little shake as if to clear his thoughts. "Daphne, I—" He closed his eyes, his forehead falling to mine. "You surprised me," he finally murmured.

"I noticed," I said dryly. "It's okay, Flynn. But like I said, I don't think we're on the same page." Shimmying out from his arms, I leaned up to press a kiss on his lips, just as Gabriel appeared in the kitchen. "I need to make breakfast."

I hurried into the pantry to the refrigerator. I needed eggs and lots of them. I also needed not to think too hard about what I'd just done. My heart was racing, and I felt a little breathless. *Feelings.* The very thing I'd thought I was well over had come roaring back, and all because of a cranky man who stole my heart when I least expected it.

As the day passed in a blur, every time Flynn and I encountered each other, I could sense the tension and concern emanating from him. I wanted to tell him to stop worrying. I really was okay with him not being where I was with us. Don't get me wrong, my heart, battered and not particularly trusting, wanted him to love me, yet if I'd learned one thing after having a marriage built on a paper foundation, it was that it wasn't worth it to try to make more out of something than there was.

That only laid the foundation for heartbreak.

What Flynn and I had was honest, and I wanted it to stay that way. Even if it hurt a little.

Chapter Thirty-Three

FLYNN

Daphne's words played on a repeating loop in my mind. My schedule was nonstop. The stolen hours I had with her at night were something I didn't want to give up. At all. I felt like a coward. Because I did love her, and somehow, I was stumbling over just getting the words out. It all felt so permanent. I feared I might ruin what we had by labeling it.

Between replaying her words, I recalled Gabriel tapping his fist over his heart and reminding me what was true and right. I was terrified I was going to let Daphne down. I was also terrified she would suddenly wake up one day and realize she just didn't want a man like me and the life I had.

Daphne—because she was a bigger person than me at heart—didn't turn me away at night. Three more nights passed until everything went wrong within the span of three minutes.

I was flying across the bay to pick up some tourists. Elias had tagged along because we had a large delivery to a village on the way. The sky was blue, and the wind was down. It was three in the afternoon because we needed to be back in time to land before sunset. Considering that it was October, that needed to happen soon.

Lucky for us, we were over land and not the ocean when a bird flew straight into the engine. I knew we were fucked right away when the engine sputtered and quit. I radioed our location immediately and stayed calm, just hoping like hell I could manage some sort of controlled crash landing.

"Hang on," I said to Elias over the rush of sound.

As I steered the wobbly plane, we hit the trees first and then landed with a loud crunch against a hillside. Blessedly, we were at a low enough elevation that there wasn't any snow. I just prayed the rescue crews could get here before darkness fell.

There was a thud in my side, enough to take my breath away as the plane settled into the ground. I closed my eyes, letting out a sharp gasp. Once I could breathe, I opened my eyes again and looked around, taking stock of our situation. My eyes sought Elias immediately. He was knocked out with a trickle of blood running down his forehead. My heart thudded in a sick beat, and worry rolled through me. I quickly confirmed he had a pulse.

A branch had punctured the window beside him. Beyond the blood on his forehead, I couldn't see if he had any other injuries from here, but his position implied it. He didn't reply when I called his name several times.

"Hang on, buddy."

Although the window was cracked, I could see clearly where we'd landed on a sloping hillside. There was snow in the distance above. There were scattered spruce trees, and the forest thickened maybe a quarter of a mile away. I tried to guess where we'd landed based on the geography around me. The plane's nose was crumpled.

This plane would not be flying again without major repairs. All things considered, I was in okay shape. One of my knees was throbbing, and I guessed I'd cracked some ribs. The door had crumpled inward when the plane landed, driving into my side.

Blessedly, I heard the distinct crackle of the radio in my headset. They knew our plane had gone down, and they had a bead on our location because the locator beacon did its job.

"We should be able to get to you in about an hour. We're coming by helicopter," the radio operator said.

"Send medical backup. My passenger is injured. Any chance I can speak to my family?" I asked.

Of course, he couldn't make that happen. However, he did offer, "You should be within a mile of a cell tower for the town nearby. You probably have reception at your elevation."

Once the stress and the immediate rush of adrenaline faded, I assessed getting out of the plane. With worry about Elias threatening to overtake me, I forced myself to think of something to stay calm. Daphne was the first person I thought of. Because I wanted to talk to her. *Now*.

Unfortunately, I couldn't reach my cell phone. It had fallen out of the spot where it usually rested between the two front seats. I could see it on the floor behind me. First things first. I needed to check on Elias from where I could see what was up with him.

"Elias," I repeated.

Silence was his only answer. Moving carefully, I unclipped my seat belt and began to see if I could get myself out of the plane. Knowing they would be here within the hour eased my worry, but it was cold. I needed to get a jacket on and a blanket to cover Elias.

A few minutes later, I'd determined it was likely the branch that knocked Elias out. He came to when I opened the passenger door. His eyes opened, glassy and confused at first.

"What the fuck?" he muttered.

"Bird flew in the engine. How do you feel?"

Elias cracked a grin. "Like hell." He started to lean forward and fell back with a grunt. "Fuck."

With a quick scan, I saw blood seeping from his side. His legs were crumpled. He tried to move again, and I spoke sharply. "Don't move. They're sending medical help. I'd prefer you stay right here. I can get some blankets on you while we wait. Moving you might not be a smart plan."

Elias opened his eyes and glared at me. "Fuck you."

His attitude eased my worry, if only a little.

I fetched blankets from the back of the plane and found my jacket. Once Elias was as comfortable as possible while also miserable, I wanted to talk to my family. And Daphne. The past few days flashed through my mind. All of my doubts about loving Daphne suddenly seemed entirely inconsequential.

It didn't matter if she didn't want the life I had and didn't want to share the burden of my family. I couldn't bear her not knowing how I felt.

Moving carefully, I circled to the other side of the plane. It took some work and the help of a broken tree branch that was lodged through the back of the plane to pry the back door open and finally fetch my phone.

My side was throbbing, and it was hard to breathe. With my knowledge of emergency first aid as an occasional backup firefighter, I feared one of my lungs might've been crushed. There was no way for me to know if there was internal bleeding.

I started to laugh, but then winced when I saw the reception bars on the phone. In so many areas in Alaska, cell reception sucked. But if you were high enough, the cell towers were mounted at those elevations. The cell reception here was excellent.

"Want to call anyone?" I asked when I returned to the pilot's seat beside Elias.

He rolled his head to the side. "Nah. Just tell everyone I'm okay."

I pulled up Daphne's name on my phone, my heart cracking slightly when I saw the name I'd given her in my contacts. *Princess*.

Tapping the number, I waited. There was no answer. She had no idea what had happened. When her voicemail came on, just the sound of her voice spun the tension inside me. I hesitated to leave a message, but I did it anyway.

"Princess, it's me. This will make sense in a few hours, and I don't know when you're gonna get this. I just needed you to know I love you. If something happens, don't forget that."

Elias spoke after I hung up. "About time."

We settled in to wait for the rescue crew.

Chapter Thirty-Four

DAPHNE

A sense of panic clawed inside my chest. "How fast can you get there?" I asked Grant for maybe the tenth time in the past five minutes.

Grant, his eyes so much like Flynn's, glanced in the rearview mirror. "Daphne, I'm driving as fast as I can."

"I know, I know," I muttered. "I'm sorry."

Gravel spit from the truck's wheels as we zoomed toward Diamond Creek.

"Hurry," Cat said from where she sat beside me in the back seat.

Nora glanced over her shoulder. "Hang tight; he's going to hit the pavement soon."

Only moments ago, we'd gotten a call from emergency services in Diamond Creek. Flynn and Elias had crashed and were being picked up by helicopter and flown to the hospital. We had only sketchy details. They were alive, the most important factor, but both had been injured. We had no idea how badly.

I needed to see Flynn. I needed to touch him, and I needed to know he was okay. My peaceful internal state I had about accepting that I needed to wait until he was ready for what we had was trampled. I needed Flynn to know I wanted nothing more than *us*.

Grant floored it once we hit the pavement. We were silent and tense in his truck for the remainder of the drive. He skidded to a jerking stop in front of the doors to the emergency room at the hospital.

"I'll park. Go on in," he said quickly.

Nora, Cat, and I ran into the hospital. Stopping at the circular desk in the emergency room, I practically barked, "We need to know the update on Flynn Walker and Elias Lowe."

The receptionist looked up with a bland smile on her face. "Are you family?"

"Yes," Cat said, her eyes snapping. "We're his sisters, and this is his girlfriend."

The woman, bless her heart, seemed entirely unruffled by Cat's frustration. She clicked a few keys on her computer and looked at the screen before replying, "They're being assessed right now. You'll have to wait. You can wait here," she explained, gesturing to the chairs lining the walls. "Or there's a smaller room down the hallway."

In silent agreement, the three of us followed the direction she pointed to the waiting room down the hallway. At first, I sat, feeling out of place and not knowing what to do. Grant eventually joined us. Nora and Grant scrolled through their phones while Cat idly flipped through magazines.

I couldn't focus on anything. I just needed to see Flynn. Restless, I stood from my chair. "I think I'm gonna go get some coffee. Does anybody need anything?"

Grant leaped up from his chair. "I'll go with you."

We walked down the hallway together and found a small refreshment station. As I was filling one of the paper cups with coffee, Grant commented, "You know, Flynn loves you."

I whipped sideways to look at him. "Huh?"

Grant smiled. "Flynn. Loves. You." He spoke slowly as if I was a small child who needed each word elucidated.

"How do you know?" My voice was shaky, and I gripped the cup of coffee. The warmth seeping through the paper to my hands barely soothed my nerves.

"Because I know my brother. Maybe he's already said it, but I just thought you should know." He reached over and slid his arm around my shoulder, giving me a side hug.

His phone buzzed at that moment. As he stepped away, he slid it out of his pocket and glanced at the screen. "Gotta take this. I'm guessing Gabriel wants an update."

As he strode away, I tried to breathe through the dread balling like ice inside my belly. I started to walk down the hallway when a door opened nearby, and a nurse pushed through. She barely glanced in my direction as she hurried past me. I kept walking slowly before I sensed motion again. This time when I glanced back, I saw Flynn.

I felt shaky all over, and my heart was pounding in an unsteady beat. I almost dropped my coffee and had to clutch it a little tighter before it slipped free from my grip.

"Flynn," I murmured, my voice coming out hoarse as I approached him on wobbly legs. His hair was damp, and his blue eyes were electric as he looked at me. He wore a shirt hanging open and a pair of mud-splattered jeans.

"What are you doing? You shouldn't be—"

Flynn stopped in front of me. Without a word, he wrapped his arms around me, tucking his head into my neck. He was cold. I could tell from the subtle tremors that ran through him.

I wrapped my free arm around him, and the coffee cup in my hand ended up squished between us. I felt a little slosh on my shirt, and I didn't even care. If he noticed, it didn't show.

We breathed together. It felt as if our bodies were actually speaking to each other.

Thank God you're safe.

I'm here.

I'm not going anywhere.

I love you.

After several moments, I lifted my head. "Shouldn't you be getting checked out?" I asked as the reality of his situation slammed into me again.

He eased his hold, and my free hand fluttered about. I smoothed his hair, which was salty and stiff, likely from the ocean breeze and the rain that had begun to fall in the past few hours.

"Did you get my message?" he asked, his eyes frantically boring into me as he ignored my concern.

"What are you talking about? No. You need to see a doctor," I ordered, fussing as I started to turn him around.

Flynn's hands gripped my shoulders and turned me back to face him. "I love you. That was my message."

My heart frantically flipped over in my chest as I stared at him. I didn't realize I was crying until concern passed through his eyes as he lifted a hand and brushed a tear away with his thumb. "That wasn't supposed to make you cry."

He folded me in his arms again, and I took a moment to absorb him, needing his masculine scent, his strength, and the sound of his heart thumping strong and steady against my ear where it was pressed against his chest to let me know he was alive and okay.

When I thought I could breathe and not be a watering pot, I lifted my head and pressed a kiss on the underside of his jaw. "I love you too," I said, suddenly feeling bashful.

His eyes held mine, the look there so intent, it took my breath away. "I'm sorry it took me crashing a plane to stop being a coward."

"You weren't a coward. I was stalling too, trying to pretend I was all cool with waiting. I'm not cool. I've never been cool."

Flynn's smile sent joy scattering through me. It felt as if the windows were thrown open into my heart, and sunshine burst through, sending light and warmth everywhere.

Flynn tolerated me running my hands down his arms and pushing his shirt to the side to see the horrible bruising on his rib cage. There was a deep contusion in one area. "Flynn." I tried to will my tears away. "You need to get checked out, and where's Elias?" I curled my hand around his.

"He's headed into surgery." Flynn suddenly looked worried and uncertain. I knew how much his friends meant to him and knew he was scared for Elias. "I think he'll be okay, but a branch knocked him out, and it looked like he had a broken leg. He was bleeding on his side, but we couldn't figure out what caused it."

"Now, where—" Just then, Cat appeared around the corner in the hallway and dashed down to Flynn the second she saw him.

Stepping away from me, he caught her in his arms, holding her securely as she exclaimed, "Flynn!"

When he released her, she was crying, and I fished

in my purse to find some tissues for her. Flynn looked dismayed at her tears.

Cat gave him an angry glare. "Of course I'm upset, you dummy. You could've died."

He tweaked her ponytail and curled his arm around her shoulders as he pulled her into his side carefully. Although he was putting on a good show of being okay, I didn't miss how carefully he moved. "I'm fine. You didn't think you'd get rid of me that easy, did you?"

"Not funny," she said before blowing her nose noisily into the tissue I handed her.

A nurse appeared in the hallway. "Ah, there you are. I figured you went to find someone. We need to run a few tests to make sure there's no internal bleeding. Now, come on."

Flynn wasn't cleared to go home for several more hours. There was no internal bleeding, though he had two cracked ribs. He refused to leave the hospital until he knew Elias was going to be okay. With Elias in surgery, all we could do was wait.

They gave us a private room that was unoccupied for him to wait with any other family and friends. Grant left to take Cat home because Flynn insisted she was going to school tomorrow and needed to go to bed at a reasonable time. Cat wasn't thrilled, but she was too subdued and tired to put up a fight. Nora had left earlier to go pick up clean clothes and bring them to the hospital for Flynn. He'd showered and changed after the medical team finished with him.

For about an hour, it was just Flynn and me waiting. The television was on a home and garden show. Flynn leaned back in his chair, rolling his head to the side. "Don't let me fall asleep. I want to be awake to hear how Elias is when he comes out of surgery."

I decided lying by omission was perfectly acceptable. I nodded. "I'll make sure you're awake."

I had no intention of keeping him awake, but I would wake him up after we got the update on Elias. I rested my hand on his shoulders, teasing my fingers lightly in his hair at the base of his neck. He fell asleep in a matter of minutes.

I had no sense of time. The cold drizzle had passed, and I could see the moon between the clouds as we drove. I had Daphne tucked against my good side and dozed off and on during the drive home. I came awake when Grant transitioned off the pavement to the gravel that was only a few miles away from home. A bump jolted my ribs, and it hurt like hell.

My breath hissed between my teeth, and I felt Daphne turn toward me. "Are you okay?"

"Completely fine," I murmured. I was annoyed as hell at my physical state. I *was* fine, but cracked ribs hurt. This wasn't my first go-round with them.

"He's fine, Daphne. He's just looking for some sympathy," Grant teased from the front.

I felt myself start to laugh and caught it just in time. "Fuck you, man. Don't try to make me laugh."

Minutes later, Grant had parked, and Daphne was walking beside me. She somehow thought she needed to hold me up. She wrapped her arm around my waist and insisted Grant carry the bag that had my filthy clothes from the accident and the usual bag I carried in the plane.

Grant tossed my things inside the living room and then gave me an assessing look. "You okay? For real."

"I'm sore, but I'm okay. For real. See you in the morning."

"Oh sure, but you're not flying anywhere. We've already rearranged everything."

"The doctor said you needed to rest," Daphne called from over in the kitchen.

Grant cast me a grin. "Daphne'll make sure you stay put." He winked and left.

Daphne approached me with something in her hand. "What do you have there?" I asked.

"Ice, for your shoulder."

I took the ice wrapped in a towel out of her hands. Striding past her, I tossed the ice in the sink. "Princess," I began as I turned back. "You're staying with me tonight. I don't need ice. I've been dosed with pain meds, and the only reason it hurt a little on the drive was because it was bumpy."

I had other things on my mind, and none of them had to do with my injuries. Daphne's hands started fluttering around me, so I stepped close and cupped her nape just before I fit my mouth over hers in a fierce kiss.

She gasped into my mouth, but her tongue glided against mine. I heard the soft catch in her throat when she sighed and softened against me.

I managed to walk her into my bedroom and close the door with my foot while I yanked at her clothes. I didn't want her to remind me I was injured, so I just kept on kissing her.

She tore her lips from mine finally, trying to swat

my hands away. "Flynn, you're gonna hurt yourself," she protested.

"I need you," I said simply.

I didn't know what she saw in my eyes, but she trailed her fingertips along my jaw. "Okay," she whispered.

She efficiently got my clothes off and ordered me to lie down on the bed. I was *all* about that.

We hadn't even turned on the lights, but the motion sensor lamp in the corner had come on at a dim setting when we came in. Her skin was golden in the shadowy light. My cock was already achy, and then she straddled me, and I felt the slick glide of her over the underside of my length. She held still for a moment. I couldn't resist leaning up to catch one of her nipples with my lips. It hurt a little because my ribs hurt like hell, but I wasn't about to let her know.

"Flynn..." She leaned forward. "Be careful."

I let my head fall back onto the pillows, looking up into her face. There was a tender gravity in her expression, and it cinched tightly around my heart.

She gave me just what I needed, rising up and reaching between us so I could slide into her silky, clenching heat. I was instantly teetering on the edge of release when she rose up and sank down once again.

"I love you," I gasped as I reached up and clumsily cradled her cheek in my hand. Her breasts were brushing against my chest, and I could feel the quickening in her body already.

"Love you..." Her words came out with a moan.

I adjusted the angle of my subtle rock into her to create a little more friction where we were joined. My hand slid between us, and I teased over her clit. Just as she bit her lip with a ragged moan, and her channel squeezed tightly, my release hit me and I cried out.

The pleasure was intense, and trying to catch my breath was not fun.

"Flynn," she murmured. She pressed a kiss to one corner of my mouth and then the other. "I gave you that one, but no more until the doctor says it's okay."

"She already did," I insisted. I *had* actually asked the doctor about this. "She just said my breathing might hurt a little."

Daphne's lips kicked up at one corner before her smile faded. On an exhalation, she dipped her head into my neck. "I was scared," she said against my skin.

I stroked my hand over her hair as my heart kicked fast and hard. "I was too. I was afraid I wasn't gonna get a chance to tell you how I felt."

Daphne lifted her head, tears glittering in her green eyes. "Don't you dare die on me."

"Not planning on it, princess."

The following morning, Cat wrinkled her nose as she stared at me, a sure sign that she was worrying about something.

"What's up?" I asked as I spread some cream cheese on a fresh toasted bagel. Aside from everything else Daphne made in the kitchen, she baked home-made bagels. We had all discovered the sheer perfection of them and no bagel would ever do other than hers.

"Am I still grounded?" Cat asked.

I glanced at the calendar hanging on the wall beside the refrigerator in our private kitchen. "If I recall, you're un-grounded officially tomorrow."

Cat let out a dramatic sigh. "I was hoping you

might shorten it by a day. After everything that happened."

I took a bite of my bagel, closing my eyes and letting out a moan. After I finished chewing, I replied, "I realize we all had a scare yesterday, but my ribs are sore, and that's about it. Is there a reason you're asking other than the usual?"

"Well, you're in love with Daphne, so I thought you might like the place to yourself tonight," Cat said, trying and failing to keep from smiling.

I couldn't hold back my laughter. "Ah, do you think I'm too distracted? Just tell me what you want to do tonight. Let's cut to the chase."

"Tara invited me to spend the night, and I'd really like to go."

I knew I shouldn't give in, but I seriously wanted to. For exactly the reason Cat said.

"Will Jonathon be there? Because that's a hard no."

Cat shook her head quickly. "No. It's just girls. You can call Tara's mom to confirm."

"I will. I won't agree until after I talk to her, okay?" Cat nodded quickly.

After another bite of my bagel, I asked, "How are you with what happened? Any problems at school?"

"No. I mean, he talked a little shit, but I can deal with it."

"Are you sure you don't want me to talk to his parents or the school?"

I tried to keep the anger out of my tone. The truth was, every time I thought about that little punk and him pressuring Cat, I wanted to bend a crowbar in half.

"I'm sure. It won't happen again. Now, I just have to figure out how to not like guys who are stupid jerks." She looked down, her cheeks flushing as she traced her finger in a meandering path on the countertop.

"Don't beat yourself up. High school isn't easy."

Cat had already moved on. "Are you going to marry Daphne?" Her eyes lifted to meet mine again.

The hope contained in her gaze cracked my heart a little. Cat missed our mom. Nora tried, we all tried, but Cat had been so young when our mom died.

My heart kicked up a racket in my chest. Because I *did* want to marry Daphne, but everything was so fresh and fragile. I sure as hell didn't know how Daphne felt about that right now.

So I gave Cat the truth. "I love Daphne, and I want to marry her. But you know she's been through a lot, so it'll happen when she's ready."

Cat bit her lip and nodded somberly. "I'll talk her into it."

I couldn't help but laugh. "Please don't."

Chapter Thirty-Six

DAPHNE

A few days later, Flynn winced as he turned to reach for his T-shirt resting on the bathroom counter. My heart gave a little squeeze in response. He was healing, but he was being a man about it and trying to pretend he was fine all the time.

My eyes traveled over the fading bruises on his side, and a shaft of fear pierced me. Not for this moment, but a memory of the moment when we got the call about the accident and the hours waiting at the hospital.

I learned this when Brandon became sick and died, but it was strange how moments could bring shocking clarity. I'd already acknowledged my love for Flynn, but I'd tricked myself into thinking I would be okay without him. The moment I wondered if his life was in danger, the urgency of my feelings became paramount.

Flynn began to pull the T-shirt over his head, and I called out from where I stood just beyond the doorway by the dresser. "Don't you need to wear your support band?"

Flynn's head whipped up, and he cast me a sheepish smile. "Fine." He reached for the support band that he was supposed to wear around his upper rib cage. He dutifully put it on and carefully pulled his T-shirt down.

He walked out of the bathroom and stopped in front of me. Tracing a finger lightly along my jaw, he dusted a kiss over my lips and then stepped back. "What are you doing today?"

"Cat wants more cooking lessons. Instead of spending the day mostly alone in the kitchen, I'll spend it with her."

"You don't mind, do you?"

"Of course not. I love hanging out with Cat. She's always funny, and she really does want to learn how to cook. You're not flying today, right?"

Pulling a clean T-shirt out of the dresser, I quickly took off the dirty one I was wearing and threw it in the hamper. Flynn interrupted me when his hands slid around my waist, and he pressed a hot kiss on the side of my neck.

"I have to get downstairs," I said as I turned in his arms.

"Well then, you shouldn't have come up here to change," he countered with a slow, belly-flipping grin.

I giggled. "I got flour all over me. Plus, what are you doing up here instead of down in your apartment?"

Flynn shrugged. "I just want to be where you are, and I woke up here. When can we talk about you moving downstairs? It's silly for you to stay up here. I want you with me every night."

"Tonight," I promised. "We already talked about it. I just need to make time to move my stuff." I stepped back quickly and finished yanking my T-shirt on. I couldn't be half-naked near Flynn and not end up tangled up with him. Cat was waiting for me in the kitchen.

"You're not flying today, right?" I repeated, keeping my tone stern.

"Nope. Gabriel is. On the way back, we'll be bringing Elias home from the hospital."

"Oh, thank goodness!" I clapped my hands together lightly. "I'm sure he's ready to be home."

"Yeah, he's a cranky ass, is what he is."

A few hours later, I was drying my hands on a towel when Cat rested a hand on her hip and leveled me with a sharp look.

"What?" I asked.

"Will you marry Flynn?"

She derailed my train of thought so completely I dropped the towel on the floor.

"What?" I leaned down to scoop the towel up. "Are you asking on Flynn's behalf?"

"You two obviously love each other, and I would like it to be official. I talked to him about it, and he's not doing anything about it, so I'm asking you."

"Cat, I'm not sure what to say."

"Well, you can tell me you're going to ask Flynn to marry you. That would be the answer I would like." Cat was so earnest my heart cracked a little for her. She lost her mother at a young age, and by all accounts, her father hadn't been much of a parent.

Despite how tight she was with her siblings, I could see Cat looked up to me and sought guidance in a way she didn't with her brothers and sister. The moment that thought passed through my mind, I almost laughed, which was kind of sad. Because of the many things I had gotten wrong in life, I thought I'd been a pretty good mother to Brandon.

I set the dish towel on the counter and crossed over to Cat. "I'm not sure what's going to happen with Flynn and me, but don't worry about it." I rested my hands on her shoulders and gave them a light squeeze.

Cat wrinkled her nose and turned to lift a ball of dough out of the bowl where it had been rising. She set it on the floured surface on the counter and punched it down before she began kneading it. In case I missed the memo, she was nervous.

"I just really like you, and you're the best thing that ever happened to Flynn. He's not a cranky ass all the time now that you're around," she said quietly.

"Good to know," I said lightly. "I promise I'll talk to Flynn. Please don't worry. I'm not planning on going anywhere, okay?"

"Promise?" Cat, for all of her toughness, gave away what a softie she was time and again.

"Promise."

———

That night, Cat was spending the night with a friend. Flynn had gotten back later than planned with Elias and Gabriel. I helped him get Elias situated in one of the guest rooms downstairs. Elias would need a little help while he was healing, much to his annoyance. He had crutches for getting around on his injured leg, and he still needed to change bandages on his side where a nasty gash had required stitches, and they'd repaired his spleen. By the time we left him, he was already nodding off in bed.

I carried some leftover pizza I'd made for the guests into Flynn's place. "Dinner," I said as I held the pan aloft and crossed over to the smaller kitchen, setting it on the counter.

A grateful look crossed Flynn's face. "Oh, thank God. I'm starving."

"You start eating, and I'll grab some beer. Any preferences?"

"A pale ale if we've got any."

Hurrying back into the main kitchen, I grabbed a bottle of pale ale for Flynn and a bottle of mead for myself. I'd gotten kind of hooked on the honey mead they made at the brewery in town. I made sure all the lights were turned off and returned to the apartment, closing the door behind me before crossing over to slide my hips on a stool across from Flynn. Still chewing, Flynn opened the drawer behind him and tossed me a bottle opener.

I passed his beer over after I opened it and took a swallow of my mead. "When's the last time you ate?" I asked when he finally paused to breathe between bites.

He cast me a wry smile. "Not since you fed me this morning."

I rolled my eyes. "You don't need to work so hard you forget to eat."

He gave a nonchalant shrug. "You reminding me to take care of myself is only one reason I need you," he said simply. The sudden gravity in his words stole my breath for a moment before my heart kicked off, drumming at a wild beat.

I waited until he finished off his second piece of pizza. There were two more to go, and I didn't doubt he was going to eat them all. Flynn ate in stages. He usually got beyond being ravenous and then paused before finishing off a meal. This was a man who loved food and savored every bite.

When he leaned back on his stool and paused to sip his beer, I said, "Cat talked to me today."

His alert gaze held mine. I tried to collect my

thoughts into something sensible. He set his beer down and leaned one elbow on the counter as he reached over to catch one of my hands in his. When I looked into his eyes, my heart went a little crazy again, tripping and stumbling before gathering itself into a thundering beat.

"Cat's impatient. I promised her I'd ask you to marry me when I thought you were ready. I'm not really sure when the best timing is, but I don't want to make myself out to be a liar. I thought maybe I could just tell you I'm yours forever. When and if you wanna make it official, all you have to do is tell me. I know you've been through a lot. I'm guessing you never meant for Alaska to be anything more than a crazy trip."

It wasn't until that last sentence that I realized Flynn was nervous. *This* man who was so confident about everything was afraid maybe he didn't own my heart.

I laced my fingers in his. "I don't want to make a liar out of you," I said, feeling my lips tug into a smile.

"What do you mean?" he asked, his eyes searching and intent.

"Oh, my God. I love you. Didn't I already make that obvious? Maybe this started out as a trip, but you're gonna have to kick me out at this point. I don't need Cat being impatient to push me to make the decision I've already made. I'm not going anywhere."

I rose from my stool and rounded the end of the counter, just as Flynn spun to face me. Stepping between his knees, I lifted my hand to cup his cheek. "We can make it official whenever you're ready."

"That was yesterday," he murmured.

I promised myself I'd never get married again. I told myself it was stupid and pointless.

Yet I hadn't counted on *really* falling in love, the kind of love that brands itself on your heart and soul, the kind of love where a piece of paper making it official gave me a sense of freedom I'd never known before.

EPILOGUE

Daphne

A year and a half later or so

"Are you sure?" Coffee sloshed over the edge of the mug when Flynn set it abruptly on the counter.

"Of course I'm sure." I could barely hear my own words over the joy rushing through me. It felt like a warm breeze, blowing the windows open around my heart.

Flynn stepped to me, lifting me suddenly into his strong embrace. His hand cupped the back of my head.

"Of course I'm sure," I repeated in a mumble into the side of his neck.

Flynn leaned his head back, his eyes sweeping over my face. "How are you feeling about this?"

This being the fact I just found out I was pregnant. We'd been trying for several months now, not in the active sense. Well, unless you count the fact that we could hardly keep our hands off each other, but that was our baseline. We'd decided to see what happened, but I refused to obsess over it and track my cycle. Because that would've made me crazy.

I took a quick breath. "I'm good. I'm really good."

Cat came skipping through the door into the living room, immediately dropping her backpack on the floor and kicking off her shoes. The second she looked over at us, she announced, "You're pregnant."

"How in the world do you know?" I mused with a laugh.

"You have a look. Plus, I can actually read Flynn's mind."

Flynn eased me down from his hold, angling to my side and keeping one arm firmly around my waist. "God help me if you can."

Cat's smile was brilliant as she skipped over to the kitchen and opened the refrigerator. "What's for dinner?"

I bit my lip to keep from laughing. The joy swelling in my heart was so immense my chest actually ached from it. "Salmon marinated in balsamic vinegar and maple syrup with asparagus and rice."

Flynn let out a moan. "Damn. When's dinner?"

Cat giggled when she closed the refrigerator and rested her hip against the kitchen counter. "I'll pass on the afterschool snack." Her gaze sobered as she looked over at us. "Are you excited?"

"Of course," I said. "We'd prefer to keep this quiet until I make it through the first trimester. Can you handle that?"

Cat made the cross over her heart and twisted an imaginary lock over her lips before tossing the imaginary key over her shoulder. "I won't tell anyone. You didn't have to tell me."

Flynn chuckled. "We didn't tell you. You guessed."

We'd actually talked to Cat about the possibility.

I'd worried about how she might feel about it. Adolescence continued to be a bumpy ride for her. She was too strong-willed and sensitive for it to be easy. She was six months shy of turning eighteen and still pushing the limits. I'd been worried that if we even considered having a baby, she might feel left out.

To my surprise, she had been one hundred percent on board with the idea and wanted me to get pregnant immediately.

"We'll let Nora and Grant know, but that's it for now," I added.

Cat bit her lip and nodded. The second Flynn let his arm fall away from me, she dashed across the kitchen and flung her arms around his neck. He caught her easily. After her fierce hug, he arched a brow. "What was that about?"

"Everything is just better. We feel like a family now."

Flynn tweaked her ponytail. "We were always a family. Do me a favor and try to get through two weeks without me getting a call from the principal."

Cat grinned unabashedly. "I'll try."

A bit later while I was getting started with dinner, Cat found her way into the kitchen as she did most days after school. Without me asking, she immediately pulled out the dough I'd prepped that morning for fresh rolls and began separating it into small balls to bake.

After a few quiet moments, her voice broke into the silence. "Are you worried?"

Sliding my gaze sideways, I found her eyes, so similar to Flynn's, looking at me with a twitch of worry between her brows.

"It would be impossible for me to say I'm not worried. Statistically speaking, any child is more likely to die in a car accident than to be diagnosed with the same cancer Brandon had. I think it'll be okay."

Cat, who'd already experienced her own share of early loss, looked back down at the dough and continued deftly dividing it into even segments.

Another moment later, she caught me in one of her fierce hugs. When I stepped back, her eyes were bright with tears. "I'm just so glad you're here."

———

FLYNN

Another seven years later

"No, you don't," Daphne said firmly.

Glancing over, I saw her curling her arm around our son's waist. He was trying to climb into the pilot's seat in one of my planes.

Charlie wiggled madly, giggling as Daphne spun him around in her arms and set him firmly on the ground. "You've got at least twenty years before you get to fly a plane."

Charlie gave her a gap-toothed smile. "You're wrong, Mama. Daddy says I can fly when I'm eighteen. That's only twelve years away."

Daphne sent me a pleading look. I couldn't help the flush of pride at how well he was doing with his math addition practice.

Crossing the concrete floor in the plane hangar to them, I knelt at his side. "Let's not worry about that now, buddy." Lifting him, I spun him in the air, effectively getting him off that topic.

Although Charlie couldn't have known what a

perfect distraction he was, Grant appeared in the doorway, and our son immediately ran over to him.

Turning, I pulled Daphne into a loose embrace with my arms looped around her waist. "He might fly when he's old enough, and it'll be fine."

Daphne shrugged. "I know." She leaned up and pressed a kiss on the bottom of my jaw.

Easily distracted by anything and everything related to Daphne, I dipped my head and caught her lips before she moved away. What I meant to be a quick kiss got hot *real* fast. Because this was Daphne, and my raw lust for her showed no signs of abating despite the years that had passed since we got together.

When my tongue glided against hers, she broke away on a gasp, her cheeks going pink. "Not the place," she warned in a heated whisper.

Ignoring her, I bent low and nipped lightly on her neck, enjoying the way she shivered in my arms. The sound of Charlie's footsteps retreated, and I assumed Grant had taken him out to look at something.

"What's for dinner?" I murmured after stealing another kiss.

"That's all you ever want to know," she teased.

"Actually, more than that, I want to know when we get a night to ourselves." I loved Charlie and having him felt like a piece of my heart was living outside of my body, but I did miss alone time with my girl.

Daphne giggled, resting her hand over my heart. "Since you're asking, Cat wants to take him up to the water park this weekend in Anchorage. Is that all right with you?"

"Fine with me. As long as it's okay with you."

Daphne was an amazing mom, the best ever. But she worried, and I knew she spent a lot of time trying not to worry. When Charlie passed the age when Brandon died, I knew that had been a milestone for her even though she didn't like to dwell on it.

"Of course it's okay. You worry that I worry. And because I know I tend to worry, I probably let him do far more than we should," she said with a rueful smile.

I pulled her close for another kiss. "Princess, you didn't answer my question."

"I'm not cooking tonight. Cat is. I don't actually know what she has planned."

I forgot that I cared. Lifting Daphne in my arms, I carried her into the office at the back, then kicked the door shut with my boot. "What are you doing, Flynn?" she squealed.

"I need a snack."

"I'm a snack now?"

I slid her hips on the desk and curled my hand under her chin. "You're not a snack, princess. You're what I need."

———

Thank you for reading Crash Into You - I hope you loved Flynn & Daphne's story!

Want more small town romance with alpha heroes & smart, sassy heroines? Evers & Afters is up next in the Dare With Me Series.

Elias is *that* guy. You know the one. Tall, mysterious, alpha and so hot it's a miracle he doesn't melt the snow on those Alaskan mountains.

He's also cranky and doesn't have time for romance.

But, he's got a soft spot for Cammi. She makes his coffee every day, and it's almost as incredible as her.

Cammi's last brush with romance was a disaster, so she's all about avoiding men. Elias is hard to avoid, but she succeeds. Until he kisses her.

Elias & Cammi aren't looking for love, but the chemistry between them is too fiery to ignore.

Their story is intense, swoony & oh-so-hot.

Keep reading for a sneak peek!

Be sure to sign up for my newsletter for the latest news, teasers & more! Click here to sign up: http:// jhcroixauthor.com/subscribe/

Elias

November

"You have a visitor, Elias," the nurse said in a cheerful voice.

I resisted the urge to actually growl at her and managed a tight smile in return. "I wasn't expecting anyone," I replied.

"Well, the coffee around here isn't the best, so I think you'll appreciate this visitor."

I didn't know this nurse's name. She wasn't one of the regulars. I'd only been here three days, and I'd already figured out the usual staff.

I closed my eyes and leaned my head against my pillows. Being in the hospital sucked. My throbbing side annoyed me, and I wanted to be out of here yesterday. Now, I had a freaking visitor. I only hoped it was someone I liked enough that they wouldn't mind me being an asshole.

"Elias?" a voice called softly.

I ransacked my brain for a moment because I knew

that voice. My weary, achy body gave itself a shake. Then, I spied her. It was Cammi Taylor. Opening my eyes, I saw her stepping into my hospital room and closing the door behind her. She had a cup of coffee in her hands, and my mouth almost started watering. Because Cammi made the best damn coffee in town. Hell, in all of Alaska as far as I was concerned. Considering that I flew all over the state and visited many coffee shops, including the high-end ones in a few cities, my opinion was based on strong research.

She turned, her blue eyes lighting up when she saw me awake. "Hey," she said as she crossed the room. "I brought you some coffee."

I sat up a little straighter in bed and silently cursed the effect Cammi had on me. Every cell in my body sat up and took notice when she was nearby. I'd been getting coffee at her coffee shop for five years now. Red Truck Coffee was impossible to miss when you drove past it on the way to the airport. It was in an old red baker's truck, a beacon representing incredible coffee and Cammi's warm smile. I started going there for the coffee, and now I couldn't be sure it wasn't Cammi that drew me like a magnet. Every time I saw her, I had to beat back my body's intense reaction.

When I first knew her, her hair was short, but she'd let it grow out and it fell in a silky bob, swinging forward as she sat down in the chair beside my bed and held up the distinctive red paper coffee cup. "Here you go."

I ignored the twinge of pain as I lifted my hand to reach for the coffee. I took a swallow, letting out a low groan at the decadent and rich flavor.

Opening my eyes, I met hers, my lips tugging into an unbidden smile. "Thank you. The coffee here is shit."

Cammi's laugh was like soft bells in the room, and I felt a tug low in my chest. "I'm sure they do the best they can, but their priorities are taking care of their patients. How are you feeling?" Her concerned eyes coasted over me.

I felt like hell, but I didn't want to complain. I hated how weak and useless I felt in the hospital.

I lifted my shoulder in a shrug. "Okay. Better now that you brought me this." I took another healthy swallow.

I tried to adjust the pillows behind me and swore when I couldn't get it right. Next thing I knew, Cammi was standing beside the bed fussing over me.

"Elias, take it easy. Here," she murmured. She leaned over me, adjusting the pillows behind my back.

I closed my eyes, taking a breath, and instantly getting a hit of Cammi—she smelled like sugar, coffee and sweetness. Jesus, this girl made me crazy.

I hated how helpless I felt, laid up in a hospital bed. I'd been arguing with the doctor about my discharge ever since I woke up here.

I was both relieved and disappointed when she moved away. Of course, she got the pillows just right so I was more comfortable.

She straightened, her face inches from mine when she asked, "Better?"

The air around us felt lit with a charge. Her blue eyes had layers of color in them, like the ocean under the sun. My eyes landed on her rosebud mouth. There I was, laid up in a hospital bed, cranky and probably an asshole, and I was a hair's breadth away from kissing her.

I didn't realize I hadn't even replied to her until I saw a flush cresting on her cheeks. "Elias?" she prompted.

Oh, right. I was too busy staring at her mouth. I brought my eyes back to hers and cleared my throat, my answer coming out rough. "Definitely better. Thank you."

Cammi sat back down. "I'll bring you coffee tomorrow too. Actually, are you getting out before tomorrow?"

I reached for the cup of coffee again, this time able to reach it easily on the table beside my bed. I needed another sip of Cammi's fine elixir. After a long swallow, I lowered the cup and let out a sigh. "I don't know."

"Well, you don't want to get out before they think you're ready," she said matter-of-factly.

"I'm ready," I insisted.

Her lips twitched, and I felt my own laugh bubbling up. I didn't want to admit it, but I knew she was right. When I finally did let a laugh loose, I followed it with a shuddering breath because it made my side hurt.

"Oh!" She pressed her hand to her heart. "I'm sorry. I didn't mean to make you laugh."

She looked so genuinely worried that I felt pressed to reassure her. "You didn't make me laugh. I'm laughing at myself. I'm just impatient to get out of here. Rumor has it I might get discharged tomorrow afternoon."

"Then, I'll definitely bring you coffee in the morning. It'll cheer you up before it's time to go." Worry suddenly crossed her features, a crease forming between her brows. "Wait a sec, are you even supposed to drink coffee? The nurse knew I had it, but maybe she thought it was mine."

Cammi started to stand from her chair, and I thought she was actually going call the freaking nurse to my room.

"I'm allowed to have coffee," I said. "Please sit down."

She said down quickly. "Are you sure?"

"Sure about what?"

Right then, the doctor, who looked young enough to be straight out of college, came through the door, his eyes flicking between Cammi and me. "Glad to see you're having visitors," he commented as he walked in.

I felt the scowl form on my face. I'd been perpetually annoyed ever since I'd landed here after the accident. I'd had a minor plane crash with my friend a few days before. He'd skated out with fewer injuries then me. I had a nasty ankle break and a doozy of a gash in one side from a piece of metal. I still thought they should've discharged me once surgery was over.

Cammi, of course, smiled. She was nicer than me. "Hi there. How is Elias doing?"

"We should be able to clear him for discharge tomorrow, assuming the check up we do tomorrow looks good." The doctor gave me a critical look. He stopped at the foot of my bed, tapping on the small computer tablet that seemed to be permanently in his hands.

When I glanced toward Cammi again—because I couldn't freaking help it—I got that usual sweet shot when my eyes collided with hers. It seemed there was nothing I could do about that.

She smiled encouragingly. "That's great. Is he taking enough medication for his pain? Because he doesn't seem very comfortable."

I practically growled at her. "I'm fine. I do *not* need anything else for my pain."

Cammi didn't need to know that I'd once come way to close to getting hooked on painkillers. I'd faced what felt like an endless desert of pain after the accident that killed a friend and landed me facing the end of my career as a pilot in the Air Force. Unrelenting with no end in sight, opiate painkillers had felt like manna from heaven, a relief from the pain and an escape from the thoughts chasing in circles in my mind.

Although the doctor here drove me kind of nuts, he seemed to understand my resistance to medication and didn't push it.

"He's hanging in there. Maybe he's a little cranky," the doctor said with a quick grin in my direction, "but not many people love the hospital. It's nice to know he's got a girlfriend who cares about him."

I almost choked. Cammi's pretty blue eyes widened slightly with a wash of pink cresting on her cheeks. She opened her mouth to reply right as his pager buzzed in the room. "I'll be back to check in later."

Just like that, he was gone. "I'll make sure to clarify you're not my girlfriend," I muttered.

Cammi shrugged lightly, her eyes coasting over my face. I hated feeling weak, I hated being in pain, and I hated that all of that was obvious to anyone who saw me. Even worse, Cammi tended to make me feel as if she could see right through me, and it drove me crazy.

"It's a harmless misunderstanding. By all means, make sure to correct him though." Her lips twisted to the side. She actually looked a little hurt, and I felt a twinge of guilt.

"Cammi, that's not it. I'm an ass and definitely not at my best in here. For that I'm sorry," I said sincerely.

CAMMI

Elias actually looked like he felt bad. Good Lord, this man was dangerous for my sanity. There he sat in a hospital bed with the sheet draped at his hips, and his hospital gown barely concealing his chest and doing a whole lot of nothing to hide the lean muscles of his arms and shoulders.

His shaggy dark blond hair was rumpled, falling almost to his shoulders on the sides. His piercing espresso eyes met mine. I took a moment to study him. His skin was burnished bronze, even in the middle of the winter. Being alone near him had my libido giving itself a shake and perking up like a cheerful puppy after a nap. It did that every time I saw Elias.

His face was a thing of beauty—cut cheekbones, and a strong jaw with a little dimple at the bottom of his chin. His rich brown eyes stood out, and oh my word, his lips were bold and sensual. Just looking at him made my mouth water a little. Did I mention he was in the hospital? His raw masculinity should've been a little weaker now. I mean, he was injured.

Of course, being Elias, the reason for him being in the hospital was no mundane accident. Oh no, even that carried an edge of sexy danger. He and his friend crashed in the wilderness in a small plane. Elias had braved cold weather and stayed conscious the entire time with cracked ribs, a broken ankle, and a nasty gash on his side, according to my friend who had given me the scoop.

Injured and in a hospital bed, Elias *still* had that crazy effect on me. Every time I looked at him, it was like getting a hit of hotness. My hormones lit up like a pinball machine, and my libido did a little dance. As far as I could tell, it was a one-way street.

I hadn't come to the hospital with designs on Elias. I'd gotten to know him over the last few years when he stopped by for coffee almost daily at my little coffee truck. Even though he was usually a grumpy guy, he was a very reliable customer and left ridiculous tips, like five bucks for a three-dollar coffee. Even if he didn't call himself my friend, I considered him part of my circle, such as it was in a small world of Diamond Creek, Alaska.

"It's okay, I know I'm not your girlfriend. I wasn't confused about that part," I teased, injecting lightness into my tone.

"I know you're not," he said, his voice coming out a little rough. "I hate being here, and it makes me more of an ass than usual."

"You're not an ass, and you'll be free tomorrow," I said, my heart squeezing a little. He looked like a lost boy. "Like I said, I'll bring coffee tomorrow for you. It'll improve your morning."

"That'd be more than nice. How are things?"

"Be careful now," I teased. "We're about to have the longest conversation we've ever had."

Elias stared back at me, just long enough that I wondered if I saw heat flicker in his eyes. Surely not. Because that was crazy thinking.

Just then, the door to his room opened again, and Flynn Walker came striding in. Flynn was another gorgeous specimen of a man, tall and lanky with dark blond hair and glacial blue eyes. There were plenty of women who pined after him.

He was a lost cause, or so I kept telling every girl who'd listen. He was beyond in love with Daphne Bell who was the chef at the outdoor resort he ran on the outskirts of Diamond Creek. I was thrilled for them.

Flynn flew planes with Elias and rumor had it they'd been in the Air Force together, along with the rest of the pilots who worked for Flynn. Flynn wore battered jeans and a navy T-shirt that made his eyes pop. He stopped beside the bed, looking from me to Elias. "Is he being nice to you?" he asked with a sly grin.

"Absolutely," I said sweetly.

"I was only a little cranky," Elias added. "I even let the doctor think she's my girlfriend."

Flynn's eyes went comically wide at that. "Damn. I guess that means she *is* your girlfriend."

Elias actually laughed, and then immediately grimaced.

"Take it easy," Flynn said.

"It's my fucking ribs, man."

"I feel you," Flynn replied, patting his own side. "You know I cracked a few. I'm still sore."

"Yeah, but you're not in the fucking hospital," Elias muttered.

"Dude, it's only been three days," Flynn said.

"Yeah, but you're free. You didn't have to spend the night," Elias argued.

"Yeah, well, I didn't get stabbed in the side with a branch and a piece of metal. You did."

Elias rolled his eyes with a sigh. "I'm gonna have a hell of a scar."

"Well, scars are badass. Right, Cammi?" Flynn glanced toward me.

"I prefer for my friends to *not* almost die," I said sincerely.

"Let me see that side anyway," Flynn commented, stepping closer to the bed.

A wash of heat blasted through me when Elias slid one arm out of his hospital gown and bared his chest and abdomen. I'd never actually seen him without a shirt. Now, I knew for sure he had a genuine six-pack, maybe even an eight-pack. My fingers twitched. Oh my God. I was getting hot and bothered over a guy in a hospital bed.

Copyright © 2020 J.H. Croix; All rights reserved.

————

Coming February 2021 - on pre-order now!
Evers & Afters

If you love hot, small town romance, take a visit to Willow Brook, Alaska in my Into The Fire Series. Check out Burn For Me - a second chance romance for the ages. It's FREE on all retailers! Don't miss Cade & Amelia's story!

Go here to sign up for information on new releases: http://jhcroixauthor.com/subscribe/

Dare With Me Series

Crash Into You

Evers & Afters - coming February 2021!

Come To Me - coming April 2021!

Swoon Series

This Crazy Love

Wait For Me

Break My Fall

Truly Madly Mine

Still Go Crazy

If We Dare

Steal My Heart

Into The Fire Series

Burn For Me

Slow Burn

Burn So Bad

Hot Mess

Burn So Good

Sweet Fire

Play With Fire

Melt With You

Burn For You

Crash & Burn

That Snowy Night - due out Dec 8, 2020!

Brit Boys Sports Romance

The Play

Big Win

Out Of Bounds

Play Me

Naughty Wish

Diamond Creek Alaska Novels

When Love Comes

Follow Love

Love Unbroken

Love Untamed

Tumble Into Love
Christmas Nights
Last Frontier Lodge Novels
Take Me Home
Love at Last
Just This Once
Falling Fast
Stay With Me
When We Fall
Hold Me Close
Crazy For You
Just Us
Catamount Lion Shifters
Protected Mate
Chosen Mate
Fated Mate
Destined Mate
A Catamount Christmas
The Lion Within
Lion Lost & Found

ACKNOWLEDGMENTS

To DBC who's there for me always, in all ways. To my family and friends who remind me what matters time and again.

Najla Qamber made magic again with this cover, and she's ever gracious with me. Thanks to my editor and to Terri D. for scouring for the details.

Many thanks to my early readers - Janine, Beth P., Terri E., Heather H., Carolyne B., Kathy C. & Lynne E.

As always, my readers. Thank you for taking a chance on my stories and for loving my characters as much as I do.

Let's remember to take care of each other.

xoxo

J.H. Croix

ABOUT THE AUTHOR

USA Today Bestselling Author J. H. Croix lives in a small town in the historical farmlands of Maine with her husband and two spoiled dogs. Croix writes contemporary romance with sassy women and alpha men who aren't afraid to show some emotion. Her love for quirky small-towns and the characters that inhabit them shines through in her writing. Take a walk on the wild side of romance with her bestselling novels!

Places you can find me:
jhcroixauthor.com
jhcroix@jhcroix.com

 facebook.com/jhcroix

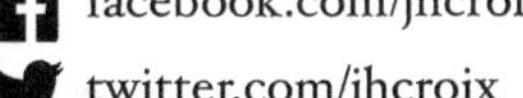 twitter.com/jhcroix

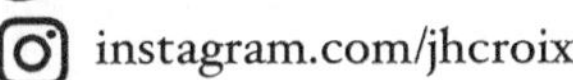 instagram.com/jhcroix

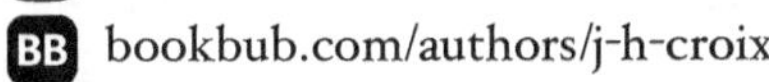 bookbub.com/authors/j-h-croix

www.ingramcontent.com/pod-product-compliance
Lightning Source LLC
Chambersburg PA
CBHW071743190726
48292CB00003B/848